**There is no such thing as magic, or sexy shifters.
Or... is there?.**

Moira Graham's car breaks down in the tourist town of Kotoyeesinay, Wyoming. She's on the run. Again. A crazy billionaire wants to possess her ability to predict the future, but it's not a "gift." It's simple guesswork. Magic doesn't exist. And this quirky town—which uses elves, fortune tellers, and fairy-tale gimmicks to draw tourists in—isn't helping.

Roving carpenter Chance McKennie is a prehistoric shifter on the lookout for a mate. Unfortunately, people fear his lion, and don't stick around long enough to get to know the man. He thought his luck would change in Kotoyeesinay, but his skills aren't needed in this magical sanctuary town with creatures of myth and legend on every block.

When Moira bumps into him, she's almost willing to believe in the magic of this place. But it's going to take more than a red-hot handyman and some glowy lights to save her from ruthless hunters.

Chance is determined to protect his mate and help her find the magic in her blood. But even a top predator can't guess the lengths to which a desperate billionaire will go to get what he wants.

Continue the magic with **Shift of Destiny,** the second book in USA TODAY bestselling author Carol Van Natta's fun, action-filled, steamy-hot Ice Age Shifters™ series.

# ALSO BY CAROL VAN NATTA

**Paranormal Romance**

- Shifter Mate Magic (Ice Age Shifters #1)
- Shift of Destiny (Ice Age Shifters #2)
- Heart of a Dire Wolf (Ice Age Shifters #3)
- Dire Wolf Wanted (Ice Age Shifters #4)

- In Graves Below (Magic, NM)

**Space Opera - Central Galactic Concordance Series**

- Last Ship Off Polaris-G (Novella)
- Overload Flux (Book 1)
- Minder Rising (Book 2)
- Zero Flux (Novella)
- Pico's Crush (Book 3)
- Pet Trade (Novella)
- Jumper's Hope (Book 4)
- Spark Transform (Book 5)
- Central Galactic Concordance Box Set Books 1-3

**Retro Science Fiction Comedy**

- Hooray for Holopticon

# SHIFT OF DESTINY

ICE AGE SHIFTERS BOOK 2

CAROL VAN NATTA

CHAVANCH
PRESS

Shift of Destiny
(Ice Age Shifters Book 2)

Ice Age Shifters™ is a trademark of Carol Van Natta

Cover and logo design by Amanda Kelsey of Razzle Dazzle Design

*Panthera atrox* illustration by Sam Salas

Published by Chavanch Press

Copyright © 2018 by Carol Van Natta

# 1

**M**oira Graham locked the door of her old, noisy, beater of a car out of habit, not because anyone sane would steal it. She was too tired and hot to sweep out the back, where barley cake pellets had fallen. It could wait until the cooler morning hours. She wiped the sweat off her forehead, then resettled her dusty ball cap over her equally dusty hair and pushed her braid back. The heat of the almost-summer June day was finally letting up with the setting sun, but her T-shirt was still clinging to her like she'd gone swimming in it.

The walk to the cozy outbuilding she temporarily called home always seemed twice as far after a long day at work. At least she had a job, even if it meant she never had a day off. That was fair, she supposed, since the dairy cows she cleaned stalls for didn't get days off, either. She slung her backpack over one shoulder as she walked up the narrow sidewalk, past the neat, white clapboard house that fronted the street.

"Moira!"

She jumped, then turned to face the elderly, dark-haired woman coming around the corner of the house.

"You've got to stop sneaking up on me like that," Moira said loudly. Del, her landlady, refused to wear her hearing aids in public because she said they made her look old. As a consequence, conversations with her involved a lot of shouting.

Del wiped her soapy hands on the dishtowel she was carrying. "I went to the sheriff's office this afternoon. You were right about that man who interviewed Emilio and his friends for that magazine sales job. The attorney general's office said he has charges pending in about five other states. He's even stranded whole teams in strange towns with no way to get back home."

"Oh no. Those poor kids." She'd overheard the guy interviewing Emilio and two other teenagers in the town's park—who conducted evening interviews at a picnic table? —and had a hunch the man was a slimeball, because his body language hadn't matched his words or his oily smiles. In the dappled shade, he'd almost looked like he had the scales of a snake. She'd mentioned it to Del, who'd started making calls. Slimeball wasn't the half of it, apparently. She shook her head. "I'm sorry the job didn't work out."

Small towns in the northeastern plains of Colorado had very few jobs for recent high-school graduates like Del's live-in grandson. Moira had lucked into her current job because she happened to know how to catch runaway cows. The barn work was exhausting, but it paid in cash under the table, which was exactly what she needed. Neither she nor her diary farm employer wanted a paper trail. Moira paid cash to rent the tiny house, because Del didn't want a paper trail, either.

Del eyed the clear bag in Moira's hand that held a

wrapped sandwich and chips. "Fast food is bad for you. Come on in. I made a big pot of chili."

Moira shook her head. "No thanks. I just need a shower and to put my feet up. I don't think I sat once all day." She didn't want to take advantage of Del's generous nature. Her landlady's only income besides social security was renting out the illegally converted shed, and she had still-unemployed Emilio to feed.

Del gave her a sly look. "You should use some of your magic and get yourself a boyfriend to give you a foot massage every night." Del knew everyone in Nunn and the surrounding farms and ranches, and had been trying to pair Moira up with anyone remotely eligible. Del had loved her husband dearly, and thought everyone should have the chance at that kind of happiness.

Moira had given up trying to tell her that any kind of relationship wasn't in the cards, and just laughed. "I keep telling you, it's not magic. I just notice things."

Del patted Moira's arm. "I understand, sweetie. It'll be our little secret."

Moira suppressed a sigh. People who wanted magic to be real never let facts get in the way of a good belief. She looked at her watch. "You're going to miss your favorite show if you stand here gabbing with me."

"You're a good girl." Del gave Moira a quick hug. "Go take your shower."

Del trundled off, leaving Moira to follow the narrow walk that led to her tiny home. At twenty-nine, Moira was too old to be called a girl, though maybe Del applied the term to anyone under fifty.

In the backyard, Moira stopped to admire Del's lovingly tended garden. It reminded her of her foster mother's garden, which had been filled with practical vegetables, but still had room for a few flowers. She missed her foster parents a great deal, but couldn't risk dragging them into the mess that was her life. All she could do was send occasional postcards and breezily tell them she was still enjoying her road trip of three years and counting. Maybe in another year, if things stayed quiet, she could finally go home again for a while.

Moira straightened her slumped shoulders, then turned and opened the screen door to the converted outbuilding.

Nothing fell.

The pink petunia petal she'd carefully placed between the door and the frame when she'd left at dawn was lying in the dirt. She picked it up and gently brushed the dust off with her thumb. The petal felt like someone had stomped on it, and incongruously smelled a bit like wet dog.

She tried the door's handle, and was relieved to find it locked as she'd left it. She let herself in with the key and pulled the door closed behind her. Sunlight streamed in from high west windows as she took in the room.

The chair at the square, battered pub table was perfectly centered under it, and the table was perfectly aligned with the strip of a kitchen. The microwave and toaster oven on the counter both squared up perfectly with the edge. The rectangular, mosaic-mirrored vase was perfectly aligned with the edge of the low bookshelf. She'd bet her sandwich that the contents of her medicine cabinet would be too neat and that the few things hanging in the repurposed school locker that served as her wardrobe were now evenly spaced.

Lawrence Witzer had not only found her, he'd been in her house and pawed through her things.

Moira allowed herself three swear words that wouldn't count toward her swear fund.

*Hell.* That was her life since meeting the man, turning

him down, and evading him ever after. She was sorry she had ever taken that summer job three years ago as a costumed fortune teller for a Renaissance fair in southern Colorado, doing entertainment tarot readings for the visitors.

Wealthy but crazy Witzer had visited her tent once and become convinced she was a genuine psychic, not just someone with common sense and a vivid imagination that had gotten her into trouble since childhood. She'd spun him a vague but colorful tale of business setbacks, intrigue, and ultimate victory over an enemy, because richly dressed customers like him tipped better when they starred as the hero of the story. She'd had no idea who he was at the time, only that he had expensive taste in jewelry and a compulsive need for order. He'd come back several more times over the run of the fair for additional readings. Then on the last day, he'd astonishingly invited her to interview for a job as a business analyst for international financial deals. He was undeterred when she admitted she only had an associate's degree in hospitality, and she'd only gotten that to please her family.

She'd been flattered by the attention and the breathtaking salary Witzer had offered, but his behavior during the meeting in Denver, in the hotel's presidential suite, was deeply weird. He obsessively straightened everything, even her sweater on the back of her chair, without seeming to be aware he was doing it. He asked her nonsensical questions about her "magical gifts," mumbled in a foreign language, and watched her like he expected her to sprout antennae or spontaneously combust. His expression made her imagine he'd soon ask to look at her ankles and teeth, like she was a prize thoroughbred he wanted to buy.

She'd told him she needed to think about it and escaped quickly, then sent him a polite email a week later declining his offer, after she'd lined up a tour guide job in Vermont because she wanted to see the fall foliage. Instead of dropping it, he'd seemed to take her refusal as a challenge, which he'd since carried to extremes. He'd overshot "eccentric" some time ago and was now well into obsessive-delusional.

*Shit.* She knew from experience that after Witzer, his goons with strong arms and black vans would soon be at her door. They'd come after dark this time, because they'd learned from their encounter last year that she could scream really loud, a skill she'd developed when she'd played a banshee in a haunted house. Something told her that if she didn't leave in the next thirty minutes, she could kiss her freedom goodbye. She was certain that Witzer, based on his unflagging pursuit, had no intention of letting her get away again.

She put her backpack on her chair and pulled out the battered rolling suitcase from the locker wardrobe. She put her toiletries in a plastic bag in the bottom, so her clothes wouldn't be ruined by leaks. Her worn athletic shoes went next, followed by her hanging clothes, then her spare pair of jeans and T-shirts, then her underwear, bras, and socks for easy access. She'd have to carry her winter coat and snow boots. She'd learned to keep her computer and cash with her at all times, so they were already in her backpack, along with her cellphone charger, hoodie, tools, first-aid kit, hair brush and small mirror, and the few important papers she had. She shoved her sandwich and chips into the top of the backpack.

In the kitchen, she pulled the can opener out of the drawer, along with one set of eating utensils and the plug-in immersion heater, and stuffed them in her backpack's front pocket. She put her only can of stew in the backpack's side pocket. She pulled the comforter off her futon and zipped it up to make it a sleeping bag again, stuffed it with her thrift-store sheets and pillow, then rolled it up. That was her entire life packed in fifteen minutes. She looked around for anything she couldn't live without.

*Fuckity fuck, fuck, fuck.* Same word, so it was still exempt from the swear fund. She really liked the quaint little town of Nunn and its residents who admired her for staying off the grid, even though they thought it was by choice rather than necessity. The dairy farm owed her a week's pay that she'd never see, and Del would be hurt that Moira didn't say goodbye. She was heartily sick of the life of a tumbleweed, blown by the wind and Witzer's demented desire to harness her supposed gifts for his benefit.

Speaking of the wind, she needed a direction. She pulled the well-worn US roadmap out of her backpack and spread it out on the narrow futon. She placed the bruised flower petal on her palm and blew it gently toward the map. It almost seemed to sparkle in the streaming late-afternoon sun, then landed. The petal's tip pointed to a mountain town on the southern Wyoming border called Kotoyeesinay. It was as good a choice as any, though the route to get there from Nunn looked convoluted. Perhaps it would slow down Witzer's hunters, trying to guess where she'd gone. If she was lucky, she could be there in a day.

## 2

Chance McKennie was doomed to never have a quiet life. His conception and birth had already been unlikely, but in his opinion, the name his parents chose to commemorate that fact sealed his fate. The more peculiar or unusual the event, the more likely he was to be nearby, or get dragged into it. Like at dinner this evening, for example, when the granite golem forgot his foot and nearly took out a table full of tourists.

Chance's favorite restaurant in the town of Kotoyeesinay, Wyoming was the Blue Fairy Diner because the chef, an actual wizard, conjured off-the-menu dishes to suit the dietary needs of her customers, however unusual.

The beast that lived inside him craved fresh, red meat, while Chance had a broader palate. Su Yen's delicious wild-game and vegetable stew was one of the few things they agreed on. The Change of Fortune Casino's June tournament meant that even on a Tuesday at dusk, the diner was hopping. He'd been happy to snag a stool at the counter, but it was just his luck, setting him up again.

He'd only taken two big spoonfuls of the flavorful stew

when he noticed the giant gray-and-pink speckled golem at a table nearby had removed its feet so its legs fit under the table while it ate its meal of what smelled like mud. It had just put one slab of a foot back on when a loud bang from the street startled everyone. Chance and most of the customers jumped or twitched, but the golem abruptly stood. Without the other foot, the golem slowly toppled, like a giant pillar of doom, toward a big booth crammed with boisterous, oblivious tourists. Chance launched himself toward the golem. Even with his extraordinary strength and speed, he could only redirect its heavy fall into the half-wall of the server station. The wall collapsed, causing the counter behind it to buckle and dump a full tray's worth of ice-water glasses on top of Chance and the golem.

Chance retrieved the golem's very heavy foot and helped it stand. The golem mumbled apologies and shoved a wad of cash at the server before leaving, but the tourists didn't even notice, since they were focused on Chance.

He wasn't surprised. The golem wore a charm that rendered it unnoticeable to ordinary human eyes. The elven town council and the permanent residents of the town made sure any visiting tourists saw or didn't see exactly what they expected. The look-elsewhere charm, issued when the town had granted sanctuary, worked perfectly for an emancipated golem. Chance, who didn't need a charm because he looked like a normal human, wasn't so lucky.

"Looks like that red-haired fella's been doing a bit too much celebratin', if you catch my drift," one of the tourists joked to the server, miming a motion that looked like downing whiskey shots. "I'll have what he's havin'." Everyone at the table laughed.

Chance pretended he was deaf as he used a wad of

napkins to dry off, then went back to his stool and his rapidly cooling stew.

Aurelio, the restaurant's manager, glared grumpily at the tourists. "They sent back a hamburger because it was too pink. Su Yen is sharpening her knives." He tilted his head toward the wrecked serving station. "I saw what you did. Thank you."

"No problem." He waved his spoon toward it. "I could do a temporary repair right now, until you can get someone in to restore it. I have tools in my truck, and don't have to be at work tonight until ten."

Though a handyman by trade, there wasn't much call for those skills in a small town full of people who could do conjuring magic. He'd have moved on before the heavy winter snows set in if he hadn't found a job at Glade General Goods, stocking after hours. The night shift had suited his unusual beast. He liked being in a community that found his shifter nature unremarkable, though that would probably change if anyone saw his other form.

It still astonished him that golems and the whole range of other creatures he'd thought were myths were not only real, but alive and peacefully co-existing in a magical sanctuary town in the middle of the Rocky Mountains. In the rest of the world, territory fights, bigotry, greed, and ancient rivalries prevailed far too often among shifters, fairies, elves, and magic users, and that was a walk in the park compared to what would happen if ordinary humans discovered their existence. Too bad he couldn't stay in Kotoyeesinay.

Aurelio smiled. It was always startling, because he looked scary, with skin too pale to be human, velvet black hair, intricate red tattoos, and metal-studded eyebrows to go with his Goth wardrobe. He wore a sanctuary illusion charm, so there was no telling what the tourists thought he looked like. "I'll take you up on your offer of a repair job, if you'll let me buy your dinner." He pointed toward the kitchen. "The back storeroom has some wood scraps you can use." He cast another baleful look toward the tourists. "I'll tell Su Yen so she doesn't use you for target practice."

Chance screwed in one more fastener to hold the temporary brace in place. He gave a quick hand-sanding to the repurposed strip molding he'd applied to keep the plywood edge from splintering, then swept up the plaster and sawdust debris. He enjoyed the opportunity to use his skills again. He missed working with his hands and building things, even if it was just a makeshift countertop. Kotoyeesinay didn't need his skills, and the town didn't have what he needed, either. His increasingly restless beast refused to wait any longer.

He gathered his tools and found Aurelio up front at the cashier station. The front door's magic spell pulsed as another customer entered. The spell felt like a variation on the friend-or-enemy type. He'd never been able to control magic himself, other than when shifting, but thanks to his mother's lineage, he could sense even the smallest use of it.

"It isn't pretty, but it's usable." He pointed a thumb toward the serving station. "You might ask whoever does the restoration to reinforce the half-wall with steel angle brackets. Whoever built it back in the day just butted it in."

Aurelio smiled. "You're a pal." Chance started to turn away, but Aurelio unexpectedly grabbed his arm and pulled him closer to speak quietly. "Don't go yet."

Chance blinked in surprise. Did he know Chance was

resigning from his job that evening? As much as he liked Aurelio, it wasn't his business or anyone else's that insistent pressure from his beast wanting to continue the search for a mate was compelling him to hit the road again. He'd initially resented the beast's nagging, but had come to admit he was as lonely as his beast. He'd hoped that in a town full of all species of shifters, he'd find a mate, but it hadn't worked out that way. If he only got one shot at the mating dance, he didn't want to miss it, so that meant moving on. "Uhm, I..."

Aurelio tilted his head toward the tiny waiting area near the door, where a single figure stood, wearing an embroidered maroon hoodie and holding a backpack, looking out into the night. A roundness of hips and the long, thick braid of dark hair suggested she was female, but he couldn't see her face. "Could you walk her to Tinsel's? Her car broke down—that was the noise we heard—and I told her I'd find her a place to stay for the night so she wouldn't have to sleep in her car."

Chance relaxed and told himself to get out of his own head. "Sure." Crime in Kotoyeesinay usually consisted of mischief by young shifters or vampires and the minor thefts reported by casino guests. In the rest of the world, smart women were understandably cautious in strange towns. "Is she a tourist?" That was code for asking if she was an ordinary human, or something else.

Aurelio gave the woman a considering look. "Well, she talks like a tourist and her aura feels human, but I think she's here for sanctuary."

That explained Aurelio's interest in helping her. His own beloved Su Yen had arrived with an entire criminal gang on her heels, so he had a soft spot for people in need of sanctuary. Usually, however, the person in question knew the nature of the town and petitioned the council immediately.

The multicultural, multi-species, peaceful community wasn't for everyone, especially those who couldn't let go of old feuds, or wanted to prey on others. Conceit, fear, and prejudice weren't exclusively human traits. The only bad things he'd heard about Kotoyeesinay were from people he wouldn't trust even in a well-lit alley. The woman's presence was a puzzle.

"I'll be careful with her, then."

Aurelio smiled broadly, revealing blood-red gums and wickedly sharp pearly teeth. "I know. That's why I waited for you." He walked around the counter and led him to the woman. "Ms. Graham, I found you a free room at a bed and breakfast called Tinsel's." Aurelio waved toward him. "This is Chance McKennie, my handyman buddy. He'll show you where it is."

The woman turned and pushed back her hood. "Please, call me Moira."

Even with a streak of grease across her forehead and exhaustion etching dark circles under her eyes, she was striking, with coppery brown eyes so wide and warm that he wanted to drown in them. Her thick, dark hair, strong nose, and flawless light brown skin spoke of an ethnic heritage as mixed as his.

The beast inside him perked up immediately and pushed him to get closer, to find out what she smelled like under the grease and road dust. Lately, his beast wanted to smell every new female he met, regardless of species. *Behave,* he ordered, *or I'll eat nothing but salads and tofu for the next week.* His beast retreated sulkily.

Aurelio handed Moira a piece of paper. "That's Tinsel's address, and the address of the business on Wizard Street I told you about that might have a job. Shepherd will move your car to his shop overnight, so don't worry about that."

Moira was already beautiful, but when she smiled, she was stunning. "You've been truly kind, and I appreciate it." She turned to Chance. "I'm not inconveniencing you, am I?" Her voice was as warm and expressive as her eyes.

He shook his head. "No, it's only a few blocks from here." He opened the diner's door for her, then followed her outside. The sun had only set half an hour ago, so the sidewalks still radiated warmth. "I'll just put my toolbox in my truck, and we can go." He hesitated. "Unless you'd rather ride?"

"No, I like walking," she said. "I want to read more of the names of the businesses. It's kind of like the aliens theme in Roswell, New Mexico, except it's fantasy elves and fairies. Oh, and psychics. 'I Knew You Were Coming Prognostication Services.'" She gave him another smile and a thumb's up sign. "Best tourist gimmick ever!" She pointed to the top of one of the aspens that lined the downtown streets. "Besides, I love looking at the color waves of twinkling fairy lights in all the trees." She shook her head. "It must have taken days and weeks to put these all up, but at least the weather is nice. I once had a job hanging outdoor Christmas lights in Chicago. Nearly froze my butt off."

Chance shrugged one shoulder. "I think they pay a company to do it." Actually, the town had traded a small plot of land to a troop of forest pixies in exchange for lighting up the trees for the summer tourists every year. The lights were conventionally solar-powered, but the color waves were pure pixie magic. Which she wouldn't have been able to see, if she were an ordinary human.

He led her to his truck, where he put his toolbox in the

locker box in back. "Do you need any luggage from your car? Where is it, by the way?"

She pointed to a mostly cream-colored, dusty four-door wagon across and down the street, under a street lamp. "I call it the Frankencar."

He could see why. It looked like it had been assembled with spare parts from a salvage yard. The main chassis was from a Subaru, but the two doors he could see didn't match the Subaru's color or each other, and the front bumper looked like it came from an old Jeep. The hood had a jagged hole that looked like something had exploded from underneath.

She glanced down. "I have everything I need for tonight in my backpack. Besides, I gave my keys to the nice man from Knight's Garage." She deftly slipped its padded straps onto her shoulders and pulled her frayed braid out from under it. "How do you pronounce the name of the town, by the way? I don't want to insult anyone."

"It's a mangled Native American place name, but it's easier than it looks. The accent's on the third syllable. Koto-*yee*-si-nay."

He pointed toward the intersection as she repeated the town's name. He purposefully shortened his steps to match her pace, because underneath her alert interest in the storefronts they passed, she was clearly running out of steam. Silence with her felt comfortable, but he found himself wanting to hear her voice again. "You're looking for a job?"

"Yeah. I'm pretty sure that hole in the hood means old Frankie threw a rod, or maybe a carburetor, if that's possible, which means a new engine. Which costs more money than I have. Hence, the job." She sighed. "I have the worst luck sometimes."

"I know what you mean." He shook his head ruefully. "I think my name is a curse."

She gave him a teasing smile. "As in, after all the good fairies blessed you with chivalry and a smoking-hot body that would make a fitness model jealous, the bad fairy twisted the meaning of your name so bad things happen to you?"

She thought he was hot? He chuckled, glad for the darkness that hid his blush. "Well, unusual things, at any rate."

"Really? Like what?"

He ducked his head, not wanting to talk about himself any more. He was dismayed to find himself telling her things he hadn't told anyone in Kotoyeesinay in the nine months he'd been there.

"No fair," she complained with exaggerated outrage. "You can't just say 'unusual things' and not explain."

He held up his hands in surrender. He couldn't tell her about any of the incidents in town because they mostly involved the supernatural residents. "Uh, last year when I was in St. Louis, I was stuck in a hospital elevator and had to help a woman give birth, because her husband passed out when he saw the first drop of blood."

"Lucky you were there to help. Did she name the kid after you?"

He laughed. "No, I think they stayed with Amelia Jane." He pointed to indicate they were turning left. "They sent me a bottle of wine, though."

"Okay, what else?"

Her attentiveness made him want to tell her tales of glory, but he wasn't a hero, just a man. Most of the time. "While I was working on a remodeling job for a high-tech company in

San Francisco, one of the managers tried to pay me to help her and her pals build a secret storeroom for stuff they wanted to steal from the company." He shrugged. "Out of eleven other contractors, they chose me." He didn't mention the part about how the woman had aggressively tried to bed him, but that to him and his beast, she smelled like death and tasted like ashes. He later found out she'd been dabbling in death magic.

"What did you do?"

"Played along until I got enough recorded on my phone, then sent the file anonymously to the company president and board of directors."

She gave him a quizzical glance. "Not the police?"

"No way." He snorted. "Knowing my luck, they'd have arrested me as the ringleader."

No one with magic or a non-human nature wanted much to do with human law enforcement, especially the more ruthless agencies that would study them, kill them, or worse, turn them into weapons. Besides, like most predator shifters, he hated cages with a passion, and police buildings had too many of them.

"Yeah, the police seem to like the easy answer." A troubled look crossed her face for a moment. His beast nudged him to find out what was bothering her and fix it, which was odd. Usually, his beast ignored humans, even pretty ones, unless it considered them a toy or a threat.

His sensitive ears heard a flurry of wings and a low-pitched, taunting squeal. He disciplined himself to keep his eyes down and not watch as a young wyvern flew by, hotly pursued by a young griffin apparently intent on catching the other's tail. Moira wouldn't see or hear them, so she'd think he was crazy.

"Huh," said Moira. She was looking up where the

wyvern and gryphon juveniles had flown a loop-de-loop before zipping off to the north.

"What?"

"Oh, nothing." She frowned and shook her head. "I'm just tired, I guess. Ever since we left the diner, things keep flickering. Maybe I need to see an eye doctor." She shoved her hands in the pockets of her hoodie. After a few more steps in silence, she squared her shoulders and gave him a too-bright smile. "You seem to travel a lot."

His beast inexplicably pushed at him to comfort her, while his human side wanted to keep her safely ignorant of things she didn't understand and would very likely terrify her. Such as, she was walking in the dark with a dangerous shifter, in a town full of even scarier creatures.

He gratefully seized on the change of topic. "I go where the jobs are. I have a temporary night job, stocking the general store. I prefer woodworking and handyman work, but it's feast or famine. Construction is a seasonal business, so I'll probably head up north for a while for the summer. Maybe Canada, where it's cooler."

She nodded. "I'd hate to work outside in the heat of the south. I worked on a framing crew for a while in South Carolina, doing hurricane repairs. Most of the crew came from up north and were happy for the work, but the spring heat was hard to take. Summer would be killer."

"You've had some unusual jobs." He winced, because it sounded judgmental. "Not that there's anything wrong with that."

She laughed. "It's okay. It's true. I don't look for them. They sort of find me. Used to drive my parents bonkers." She shrugged one shoulder. "I'm not cut out for nine-to-five in a high-rise." The troubled look was back on her face, deeper this time, with a hint of fear thrown in.

He tried for safer ground. "Sounds like you travel a lot, too."

"Sure do." Her tone was genial, but her expression blanked, giving him the impression she didn't want to talk about it.

As usual, he was bungling his end of the conversation, which always happened when he was around an attractive woman. Except she was actually moving closer instead of edging away, so her discomfort didn't seem to be about him. Maybe it was the traveling. Maybe it wasn't her choice, any more than it was his.

He'd left his very rural home in the Yukon Territory of Canada when he was seventeen. It was bad enough that his wily wolf-shifter father and rare magical cougar-shifter mother had defied their respective clans to come together as undeniable true mates and conceive a child, which, according to their oral histories, was supposed to be impossible. They would have been left alone if their miracle child had fit in. When the jealous, insecure leaders on both sides discovered that Chance's beast was neither a wolf nor a cougar and couldn't be dominated by either, his very existence endangered everyone he loved. Sooner or later, he'd have had to kill or be killed.

So he'd left. He'd knocked around an endless parade of big cities and rural communities throughout North America since then, adding construction skills to the woodworking techniques his father had taught him, and going where he could find jobs. He'd saved a lot of money because he couldn't think of things to spend it on, other than his truck and tools. Thanks to a magical driver's license and passport his mother had supplied, he never had hassles with immigration authorities in any country. He missed his parents and hoped they were doing well, but even sending them a postcard would be too dangerous. Their continued safety depended on him not being a wild card in pack or pride politics.

When he'd turned thirty a couple of years ago, his beast had begun looking for a mate with ever-increasing imperative, driving Chance to keep moving even more than he had. He had no idea if that was usual for his kind, since as far as he could tell, he was the only one of his kind. He knew his human social skills were rudimentary, a result of his itinerant lifestyle and independent nature. He wasn't the type of man or beast a woman would be proud to take home to meet the family.

They turned another corner, and he pointed to Tinsel's three-story, miniature castle of a house, complete with crenelated towers and granite-block exterior. It was decorated with year-round Christmas lights. Thousands of them. In summer, the house put theme-park palaces to shame. In winter, it could probably be seen from orbit, despite the surrounding cover of evergreen trees.

Moira gasped, then closed her slack jaw with a snap. "Wow." Her steps slowed. "That certainly explains the name."

Tourists assumed the owner was just fond of Christmas. Locals knew that Tinsel was a polar fairy, with decorations she'd collected from winter celebrations all over the world. When she'd discovered Chance's woodworking skills, she'd hired him to build and decorate a miniature wooden sleigh that she used to get around town, since anything but sub-freezing weather was too hot for her to walk in for long. Powered by her magic, it behaved like the scooters he'd seen disabled folks using in the mundane world.

Tinsel herself greeted them at the door wearing a

glittery red and green gauzy cloak. "Welcome, dearies, welcome!" She opened her arms wide and ushered them in.

Chance sneezed as he closed the door behind him and felt the magic of her wards adjust to the new visitors. As usual, the scents—mistletoe, frankincense, myrrh, nutmeg —nearly overwhelmed his enhanced sense of smell. His beast urged him to put a paw over his nose and go outside, but he refused to hurt Tinsel's feelings.

"You have the most amazing house I've ever seen," said Moira, her eyes wide with wonder as she took in the elegant, one-of-a-kind decorations that framed the wide entryway.

"Thank you, dearie." Tinsel pulled Moira in for a quick hug. "I know it's a bit much for *some* people"—she gave Chance a pointed look—"but it makes me happy."

Moira turned in a circle, laughing. "I love it." Her energy enveloped him like a whirlwind, with an undercurrent of latent magic so subtle, he wasn't sure it was really there. Everything about her drew him like a magnet, but if she wasn't a potential mate to him and his beast, sooner or later, he'd have to leave. Better not to start something he couldn't finish.

And that wasn't even counting the whole revelation about the hidden magical world, or the beast under his skin. He wanted to stalk her, then catch her and kiss her until they both forgot everything but each other. Adrenaline and desire flooded his system.

A cuckoo clock in the entryway chimed three times, reminding him that he was out of time. "I'll leave you in Tinsel's capable hands." He stepped backward toward the door. "Good luck with everything."

He opened the door and fled.

## 3

"More pumpkin bread, dearie?" asked Tinsel. She held out the basket of still-warm slices.

Tinsel's house in the daylight was no less astonishing than it had been the night before. Eclectic ethnic decor from many cultures blended together to create a wonderland of a home. The open-space architecture saved it from feeling cluttered.

Moira shook her head. "No, I'm stuffed." It was the first full meal she'd had in days. She'd been the only guest for the night, and she felt guilty eating enough for three, but Tinsel was a phenomenal cook. Moira decided that Tinsel was one of the world's cheerful people, which was a delightful change from surly gas station attendants and suspicious convenience store clerks. And overnight, someone had thoughtfully dropped off her suitcase from her disabled car, so she'd had her whole wardrobe to choose from—four clean blouses and two pairs of jeans—to dress for job hunting.

Moira carefully folded the real linen napkin and placed it on the table. She'd been afraid to actually use it, so she'd surreptitiously wiped her fingers on her jeans. "Since you won't let me pay you for a night in the Lost Princess room, could I at least wash the dishes or something?"

Tinsel patted her hand. "No need, dearie. The low-country elves come in and do for me every day."

Moira smiled. "That's a great name for a house-cleaning service."

"No, they're, er... yes, it is." Tinsel turned and headed to a Victorian-style breakfront desk, where she riffled through one of the cubbyholes. "Here's that map you asked for."

"Thanks." Moira stood and crossed to take it, rather than make the woman walk any more than was necessary. "I don't know why my phone's map only shows the one street on the edge of town."

Tinsel waved plump fingers dismissively. "The town likes it that we're not worth bothering with. I'll be back in a minute." She waddled off through the kitchen toward a door that Moira assumed led to her private space. A blast of cooler air blew in when the door opened and closed. She'd have thought living in a high mountain town would have made air-conditioning unnecessary, but maybe rich guests expected it.

Moira returned to the dining table and spread the map out. For a moment, the words and lines seemed to waver, but then settled down. She was probably still tired from three long days of traveling, having to baby her balky car along mountain roads, getting lost once, and shivering in the back of the wagon each night while trying to rest. Not to mention, last night's vividly erotic dreams about the deliciously attractive handyman, Chance McKennie, in his faded black jeans and grass-green T-shirt that lovingly outlined every fascinating chest, shoulder, and arm muscle. He pushed buttons she hadn't known she had.

She'd seen dozens of well-built, handsome men in the nude when she'd wrangled props and kittens at a photo shoot for a "Real Men With Cats" charity calendar four years ago. She wouldn't have minded sexy-times with some of them, but they were candles in the wind compared to the blazing hot bonfire that was Chance.

She'd never felt anything like it, and certainly not within twenty seconds of laying eyes on a man. She wanted to run her fingers through his wavy red hair to see if she could feel the heat. She wanted to trace his proud cheekbones and chiseled jaw with butterfly kisses, and feel his short beard on her skin. She wanted to taste him, and memorize his biceps and thighs, and grab handfuls of his nude-sculpture-worthy ass. She wanted to explore all the sensuous, sensitive parts of him with her lips and tongue, and she wanted him to do the same to her. It had been all she could do to carry on light conversation with him during the walk from the diner, and not babble like she was tipsy or rub herself on him like a cat claiming ownership.

It would have been easier to ignore her out-of-control hormones if he hadn't been such a down-to-earth man. He clearly had no idea that he could have as many lovers as he wanted, and probably wait-listed a few more for emergencies. Which put him completely out of her league. She was toned but fleshy, her face was more lively than pretty, and grand romantic gestures made her laugh. Men never lined up at *her* door, unless she counted Witzer's minions. Even if she were the type to have an exciting erotic affair with a near stranger who would probably soon be leaving, she might have to leave even sooner, or he'd become collateral damage in Witzer's crazy quest to gain command of her "magic."

It was just as well that Chance had taken off

immediately after delivering her to Tinsel's doorstep, or she might have been tempted to ask him for a date, or if he wanted to practice water conservation and shower with her that evening. Which reminded her of last night's embarrassing discovery that she'd been wearing engine grease on her face like it was camouflage paint, her hair was filthy, and her clothes smelled like gasoline and stale hay. No wonder the man had run away.

She shook her head and refocused on the map, tracing the route from the diner to Tinsel's, and from Tinsel's to the job-lead address that Aurelio had given her last night. Knight's Garage, where Shepherd had promised to take her car, was only two blocks to the north. The town felt bigger than it looked on the map, but she hadn't seen much before Frankie's engine had exploded so dramatically. It was a small miracle that no one had taken it for a gunshot and returned fire.

She pulled her cellphone out of her pocket and took a quick photo of the area of the map she needed. The camera's flash made the map seem to sparkle for a moment. Well, it was a promotional-style map, so it'd be in keeping with the town's theme to add a little micro glitter to the printing ink. She refolded the map and left it on the table. The town's marketing committee deserved a national award for attention to detail.

Moira pulled on her hoodie against the morning chill, checked that she had her phone charger, then zipped up her backpack.

"Oh good, you haven't left yet." Tinsel waddled over to Moira and handed her two cards. "This one is for the front door's card reader. Just like the rooms at the casino."

Moira handed it back. "Thank you, but to be perfectly frank, I saw your rate card on the door this morning, and I can't afford to stay here even one night." She'd enjoyed most of her odd jobs, even some of the underground ones she'd had while on the run, but none of them paid anything close to what it would take to stay in Tinsel's bed and breakfast.

"Hush, dearie." Tinsel put the card back in Moira's hand. "That's just the rate I charge the tourists and the gamblers so they think they're special." She patted Moira's hand. "I'll take whatever you can pay."

Moira didn't want to be ungracious, so she gave up the fight, but vowed to find some way to pay or trade for what the room was worth. She looked at the other card. "Er, this is a get-out-of-jail free card, signed by 'Sheriff Stands On Rock.'"

Tinsel laughed. "Isn't it great? The town sheriff gave them out as Christmas gifts last year. I ran out of business cards, and it's all I could find to write my phone number in case you need it. I also gave you Chance McKennie's cell number." Tinsel waggled her silvery eyebrows suggestively. "In case you need a man who's good with his hands."

Moira chuckled and fought off a blush. "Thanks, but I don't think he's interested."

Tinsel laughed again. "He's a little slow on the uptake sometimes, but he'll come around." She lowered her voice conspiratorially. "You might need to civilize him a little."

Moira smiled, thinking that was the last thing she'd want to do to him. He struck her as someone who could use the freedom that a little wildness brought. She slid both cards in her shirt pocket and patted it. "Thank you for these. I'm off to seek my fortune. Well, minimum wage, at any rate. Wish me luck."

Tinsel put her finger alongside her nose. "May you find your magic and luck when you need them most." An errant breeze animated Tinsel's hair, and then Moira's.

She smiled at the sentiment, and accepted the wish in the spirit it was given. Maybe everyone in the town of Kotoyeesinay was a little nuts.

She stopped abruptly in the middle of the sidewalk when she saw the name of the business Aurelio had sent her to, Turn of the Cards. Moira didn't believe in signs and portents, but considering that turning tarot cards put her on the runaway train that was her life, it gave her pause.

On the other hand, a job was a job, and she needed the money for immediate transportation out of town if, or more depressingly likely, *when* Witzer found her. She took consolation in the fact that on the walk from Tinsel's, she'd seen a dozen businesses advertising everything from psychic readings and séances, to a Hobgoblin Accounting Service, all in keeping with the town's tourist theme. Maybe Kotoyeesinay was the summer home for psychics and magical entertainers, sort of like Florida used to be for circus performers. If Witzer did track her to Kotoyeesinay, with luck, he'd be slowed down by the distraction of shiny new psychics to try.

She shook off her doubts, squared her shoulders, and made herself go up the steps to the tall, two-story, Swiss-style chalet with a steep, decorated roof, and red-and-white detailing. It was well kept, with classic 1920s construction details, which made her wonder how old the town was. It had the most eclectic mix of architectural styles she'd ever seen.

Turn of the Cards turned out to be a bookstore and gift shop that specialized in all things psychic, with an emphasis on divination cards. Shelves, tables, and antique display cases showed off crystals, wands, and pyramids, plus a dazzling array of jewelry. The store carried at least twenty different tarot decks, from the classic Rider-Waite to modern, limited-edition decks by modern fantasy artists. She admired the skill and patience it must have taken to create seventy-eight steampunk paintings to make up a deck. The orderly display arrangements drew the eye but didn't overwhelm. The impressive book section had a couple of soft chairs to make it cozier. The store was neither too hot nor too cold. It took her a few minutes to realize it was deserted.

She threaded her way to the antique-glass sales counter with the modern digital pay station. A thick curtain of beads hung in the frame of a doorway behind it. "Hello?"

"Coming," shouted a man's voice from within.

She heard footsteps on stairs. Suddenly, a little white kitten burst through the beads and ran at light speed toward the store's front door. Fortunately, she'd closed it after letting herself in, or the kitten would have been halfway to the highway by the time an elderly man with round glasses and a shock of white hair made it to the counter. "Pandora! Come here at once."

The kitten pawed a couple of times at the door, scampered sideways, then made a beeline for Moira's feet. Instead of diverting at the last second, Pandora launched herself up Moira's pant leg and used her needle-sharp claws to climb higher. "Oh no you don't." Moira caught the little terror before her hoodie or her favorite red-paisley blouse got permanently ventilated. The kitten mewed twice, then relaxed when Moira nestled its soft, warm body into the crook of her arm. She tickled the kitten's belly, and was rewarded with play bites.

"Please accept my apologies, madam." His British accent

went well with his maroon damask smoking jacket and brown velvet pants. "Mr. Houdini would envy her escape-artist talents."

Moira laughed. "She's precious." She tickled Pandora's belly again and let her gnaw on the tip of her little finger. "I think kittens only have three speeds. Sleep, eat, and warp factor ten."

"You're familiar with the species, then," he said indulgently. "How may I help you?"

"Are you Mr. Maxen? Aurelio at the Blue Fairy Diner said you might have a job opening."

He nodded. "You must be Ms. Graham. I am indeed in need of help with the shop." The corner of his mouth twitched. "And kittens."

Moira was touched to realize Aurelio had gone to all that effort for her, a perfect stranger. "I'm a good worker and reliable, and I know something about the tarot decks, but I have to be honest with you, I don't believe in any of the supernatural stuff in this shop." Moira lowered her voice to a confidential whisper. "I'm not sure I'd be a good salesperson."

Mr. Maxen gave her an amused look. "I don't believe in it, either."

"Huh," she said, nonplussed.

"Fortunately, the customers don't seem to notice. They usually already know what they want." He fixed her with a direct gaze. "And what do you want, Ms. Graham?" A glint from his glasses dazzled her momentarily.

She considered giving him a vaguely pleasant answer, but she had the feeling it would annoy him. "To make enough cash to buy a new engine for my car, so I can leave."

"Nothing permanent, then." He frowned.

She sighed and shook her head. So much for this job.

"No, sorry. I'm just passing through." She needed a couple more random stops like Kotoyeesinay to throw off her pursuers. Too bad, because she liked Mr. Maxen, even though she'd just met him, and thought she'd have enjoyed working for him. For some reason, she felt like she owed him an explanation. "The last time I got mixed up with fortune-telling, it brought me a load of trouble. I need to keep moving." Little Pandora had become a boneless, snoozy fluffball in her arm. "What should I do with your kitten?"

"Would you mind terribly if I asked you to come in the back with me and put her in her bed? She behaves far better with you than me."

"Sure." She walked slowly around the counter, taking care not to knock anything over with her backpack. Mr. Maxen pushed aside the beads for her, then pointed to a mahogany 1930s Art Moderne desk with a round hatbox on top that contained a cushion covered with a leopard-print blanket. She gently slid the kitten from her arm onto the soft blanket. Pandora stretched her tiny pink toes and claws out, then relaxed into slumber.

The office area looked like it might have been the house's original central hallway, with stairs leading up. She touched the edge of the warm brown wood of a stair tread, admiring the matching baluster and handrail above it. She imagined the front sales floor had once been the living room, dining room, and parlor. With the bedrooms upstairs, it would have been a cozy house for a young family, back in its day. If she'd had a more normal life, or at least, didn't have an obsessed billionaire chasing her around the country, she could see herself lovingly restoring an old house like this one. Maybe she could hire a hot handyman to help her. She laughed at her fancy.

She turned to go, only to find Mr. Maxen giving her a speculative look. He opened his mouth to speak, only to be interrupted by a ringing phone, a buzzer, and a tinkling of bells that meant the store's front door had opened. Laughter and voices suggested the retail area now had multiple customers.

Mr. Maxen looked both exasperated and slightly overwhelmed.

Moira needed to keep looking for a paying job, but she could stay for a little longer. "I know you don't know me, but would you like me to go out front, just to keep an eye on things until you get there?"

He sighed. "Yes, if you would."

She started for the doorway, then stopped long enough to drop her backpack under a tall mirror with a gilded frame. The hallway felt safe enough, and customers would think it strange if she wore a backpack while minding the store. At least her mirror-embroidered hoodie fit right in with the decor. Mr. Maxen picked up the phone and answered it as she pushed her way through the curtain of beads.

She used crossing to the entrance to make sure the front door was closed as a cover for taking a quick headcount of the three adults and two children who were now wandering the store. The balding man with glasses made a beeline for the bookshelves, once he saw them. The two round-faced, plump women looked enough alike to be sisters, and they chatted easily as they stopped at anything shiny. The two boys, who were maybe ten and twelve years old, looked disgruntled, as if they'd hoped for cheesy puffs and had gotten carrots instead. They needed entertainment, or they'd make their own, at the expense of the store's beautiful displays.

"Hi," she said to the two women as she walked back toward the counter. "Could I enlist your children to help look for a kitten? She might be hiding in here somewhere, and she'll cause trouble if we don't find her."

The woman in a robin's-egg blue summer dress turned to the boys. "Ethan, Noah, help the lady find her kitten." She gave them a warning look. "Look with your eyes, not your hands."

Moira smiled at the boys. "I really appreciate it. She likes to hide in low spots. She's small and fluffy white." She cupped her hands together to indicate the kitten's size. "Her name is Pandora, and she might come to you if you call softly. Loud noises scare her."

"What do kittens smell like?" asked the younger boy earnestly.

Moira blinked. "Er, like fur and cream, I think." She'd seen a small saucer on the desk in the back.

The older boy turned to his brother. "Let's crawl. We have to think like cats, like Amnon and Nasir." The boys dropped to their hands and knees and started looking in low shelves.

"She can't eat us, can she?" asked the younger boy.

"Nah, we're too big," the older boy said.

Moira smiled at the whimsical conversation.

"Excuse me, ma'am," said the other woman in a day-glow pink top and yellow shorts, "but do you have any geodes?"

Moira wasn't exactly sure what one was, but it sounded mineral-like. She pointed toward the east wall. "Check near the crystals."

She retreated behind the sales counter, before more questions revealed her ignorance. Movement flashed in her peripheral vision, and she discovered an ornate mirror hanging near the ceiling that she hadn't noticed before. When she looked around, she saw Mr. Maxen had strategically placed several other antique mirrors at varying heights, meaning someone standing behind the counter had a good view of most everything in the store. The one that had first caught her eye gave her a view of the books area, and for a moment, some distortion in the old mirror made the balding man look like an upright version of Smeagol from the Hobbit movies, except with shiny gray skin and a long beard, but he looked normal after she blinked.

Uneasily, she wondered if the vision problems she'd been having were a symptom of something more serious, like a brain tumor, causing hallucinations. Maybe she should pick a larger city for her next landing spot, one that had an emergency room in a big hospital. Not that she had money for treatment, but knowing would be better than worrying. If it was terminal, she thought with black humor, maybe Witzer would finally leave her alone.

By the time the adults were ready to buy, the boys had looked in every nook and cranny of the store for the "missing" kitten, who was still safely zonked out in her hatbox bed when Moira went to find Mr. Maxen so he could ring up the sales.

He was just coming from the back, so he handed her the box he was carrying and asked her to put with the others, pointing with his chin toward a hidden storage area under the stairs. He brushed dust off his smoking jacket and went out front.

Moira stacked the box on top, then latched the door to prevent a certain white furball from sneaking in. She gave the sleeping kitten one last, soft stroke, then retrieved her backpack and settled its comforting weight on her shoulders. She checked her appearance in the hall's slender mirror and smoothed back the curly escapees from her braid. Someday, she'd like to be able to afford to have a professional haircut again, instead of borrowing office scissors.

Maybe she could find a job that kept her out of sight, making it less likely for Witzer's goons to stumble across her if they happened to come through town. She couldn't think why they would, but she hadn't expected they'd find her in Nunn, either.

She envied Chance his graveyard-shift job that was indoors. She made a mental note to ask about a position at the town cemetery. She had experience with both landscaping and tombstone carving from previous short jobs.

The front-door bells tinkled multiple times, signaling several new customers. She was glad that Mr. Maxen's little shop seemed to be doing well, despite being a couple of blocks off Glade Street where most of the tourist shops and restaurants were. She hoped he'd find the help he obviously needed. She turned to dive through the beads, only to nearly run into Mr. Maxen.

"Oh, you're leaving, then?" he asked. His expression seemed to say he didn't know if he liked the idea.

"Yes, I need to find work." She stuck out her hand. "It was nice meeting you, and if I run into anyone looking for a job like this, I'll send them your way."

The front-door bells tinkled again, and a loud voice boomed through the store. "Hello, Iolo! I brought that bus full of tourists I've been promising." The Slavic-accented male voice sounded irrepressibly hearty.

Mr. Maxen rolled his eyes in exasperation, then gave a resigned sigh and caught her gaze. "Ms. Graham, you're hired."

Moira blinked. "But you wanted a permanent employee..."

"Apparently not," he said. At her puzzled look, he added, "You're here just in time." He waved toward the front of the store. "I have more customers in here today than I had all last week. Either the Goddess of Life is giving me a cosmic hint, or you bring the store good luck. Either way, it would be foolish to let you get away."

Moira shifted her weight uneasily. The hint of possessiveness made her uneasy. Witzer claimed she brought him luck, too, and look what kind of trouble that brought. On the other hand, Iolo Maxen seemed sane and kindly, and obviously could use the help. "How about you just hire me for today, and we see how things go?"

"Iolo!" The cheerful-voiced man sounded closer and louder. "Get your ancient bones out here and give your younger and much handsomer friend Sergei a proper welcome!"

Mr. Maxen nodded. "Agreed. Put your pack and jacket under the desk and come out front."

Ten hours later, Moira gratefully wallowed in one of the compact stuffed chairs in the store's book section. Her sorry feet competed with her aching back for the title of most unhappy, but at least the busy day had gone by quickly. She was also grateful that the disconcerting flickering in her vision seemed to have finally tapered off. Sergei's busload of tourists had been followed by steady stream of customers all day.

Mr. Maxen had been right about the customers knowing what they wanted, and no one seemed to notice or care that she had no idea which gems were supposed to be used for what, or the best chime sequence for achieving astral projection. Some took delight in explaining the antique occult items, and she took delight in selling them. At the end of the day, Mr. Maxen practically had to shove the last stragglers out the door, twenty minutes after the seven o'clock closing time, so he could dim the front lights and set the modern-looking alarm.

Pandora had alternately been playful, curious, and skittish, as was the whim of kittens, and was currently lying on her back, snoozing in the valley of Moira's thighs. She envied the kitten's boneless contentment. Not to mention, its full belly. Her own complained about probably missing dinner. She'd only had a couple of pickled eggs for lunch from the gas station a couple of blocks away. Small-town grocery stores usually closed early, and anything but going back to Tinsel's felt too far to walk. While she'd secretly been hoping to run into insanely hot Chance McKennie, she couldn't afford to be eating out any more, or starting a relationship with a man who was as rootless as she was. A life on the run was full of little sacrifices.

She'd forgotten to discuss a salary with Mr. Maxen, and hoped he'd agree to minimum wage for the ten hours. Some people got stingy when they thought they had the advantage, like the greasy slob who'd tried to short her and the undocumented Mexican lady who cleaned his truck-stop motel rooms. She doubted Mr. Maxen was like that, though. If he paid her cash, she could go straight to Tinsel's and offer a token payment for her smallest room, then crash. She was unaccountably tired, as if she was fighting off an infection. She hoped it was just stress, because summer colds were the pits.

She lifted the kitten to her shoulder to snuggle her as

she walked toward the office. Pandora nuzzled Moira's neck and tried to suckle on her earlobe. Once on her little bed, Pandora curled into a white ball of fluff and covered her face with a tiny paw. She wondered if the kitten lived in the store. Or for that matter, if Mr. Maxen did.

He appeared in the wide, wood-encased doorway that led to the back of the house. It had what looked like hieroglyphics carved on each side. He beckoned her, with a wave, then brushed a few of the hieroglyphics, as if dust had gotten in them. "Come with me so I can pay you."

She grabbed her backpack and hoodie from under the desk and followed, interested to see more of the house besides the sales floor, office, and the small customer bathroom. As she passed through the doorway, she admired the detailed carving of the hieroglyphics. She remembered something about Egyptian decor being a fad in the 1920s after the discovery of King Tutankhamen's tomb.

The back area proved to be noticeably cooler and had little natural light. It had a modern, open kitchen area and a widened back door that had been converted to a loading dock with a lift-door. The rest looked like a giant workroom, with multiple benches with tools and low shelves filled with an eclectic assortment of mundane and exotic... artifacts was the best word she could come up with. Some looked like props from a fantasy movie, like magic wands and crystal orbs. Others looked like exquisite antiques, including an intricate, pierced-metal lantern. Another area seemed to be reserve stock of souvenirs for out front. It reminded her of the back room of a small appliance repair shop, but neater, as she would expect of Mr. Maxen.

After a few steps into the big work area, though, the flickering lights at the edges of her vision came back. She squinted, which seemed to help, until she accidentally brushed her fingers against an ornate, empty picture frame. Light flared suddenly from the frame, with an afterimage of a small pack of black wolves on the trail of a distant fleeing figure in red and blue. She cried out and stumbled, putting her hands up like blinkers to block the lights.

"Are you feeling well, Ms. Graham?" Mr. Maxen turned from the old Victorian desk to look at her. He'd refused to call her Moira, even though she'd invited him to do so several times. She'd whimsically decided he was old school, when men didn't casually call women by their first names, and had treated him with corresponding deference, so as not to make him uncomfortable with her forward, modern-woman ways.

She resisted the urge to rub her eyes, because it didn't help. "Just hungry, I think." She smiled gamely. "It's been a long day."

He raised an eyebrow, as if he knew she was fibbing, but didn't call her on it. "It's my fault you had such a poor lunch, so I added a bit extra to pay for your supper." He handed her a cream-colored envelope.

When she looked inside, she gasped involuntarily, then thrust it back at him. "I think you gave me hundreds instead of tens."

"And so I did," he said firmly, making no move to take the envelope. "Fifteen an hour, plus commission, plus dinner."

She shook her head, which was a mistake, because the pain behind her eyes was getting worse. "I can't take this much. I didn't earn it." It brought up unpleasant memories of Witzer upping the salary offers to ludicrous amounts, as if that was all it took to convince her to work for him. She took one of the hundred-dollar bills out and put the envelope on the desk, since Mr. Maxen had clasped his hands behind him. The peripheral flashes were nearly constant, and it felt like the walls were inching closer. "Which way should I go out so I don't trip your alarm?"

He tilted his head, then dropped his gaze. "I see I've offended you, which wasn't my intention. Turn of the Cards had its best sales day all year because of you." He moved gracefully to the widened back entrance and pressed an eight-digit sequence into the alarm's keypad, then raised the door.

She moved quickly. She didn't want to be rude, but she had to get out of the workroom immediately. A wave of summer heat made her flush, and she blinked to see the bright sun, still a half an hour away from setting behind the mountain peaks. For some reason, she'd thought it would be fully dark and almost winter. Her wayward imagination was always getting her in trouble. She shook her head, laughing ruefully at herself as she slid the money into her buttoned chest pocket and turned back to him.

"I'm sorry if I offended *you*." She draped her hoodie over her arm and settled the familiar weight of her backpack on her shoulders, relaxing into the outdoor warmth and light that seemed to drive away the strobing flashes. "If you're still okay with hiring me on a short-term basis, what time should I come in tomorrow?"

He crossed his arms. "I will pay you one hundred and seventy-five a day in cash plus lunch, which I will send you to fetch for both of us. We're closed on Mondays. If that is acceptable to you, please be here around eight forty-five so we can open at nine."

The high salary for a simple retail sales job in a small town pushed the boundaries of her comfort zone, but she desperately needed a new engine for her car, or she'd be a sitting duck. She made a private vow to be the best damn employee he'd ever had for as long as she stayed.

"I'll be here on time." She glanced down at her plain button-down blouse, jeans, and worn athletic shoes, then at Mr. Maxen's elegant smoking jacket and velvet pants. "I'll try to wear something a little nicer." Maybe the town had a thrift store.

"Your present wardrobe is satisfactory, Ms. Graham. It puts customers at ease." He brushed the satin lapel of his jacket and gave her a sardonic smile. "I have a reputation as an eccentric to uphold."

She gave him a teasing grin. "Well done, then."

He laughed. She turned to look at the small backyard and the alley behind. Most of the yard had been sacrificed to the wide driveway for trucks, but little strips of alpine garden, complete with natural rock troughs filled with delicate flowers and low shrubs, made charming borders for it. "How do I get back to Wizard Street from here?"

Mr. Maxen gave her directions for a shortcut to Tinsel's, then retreated into his store and pulled down the loading dock door.

Her sore everything complained as she walked down the alley, making her remember her former landlady, Del, teasing about finding a boyfriend to rub her feet.

Moira was tired of making friends and losing them, afraid of even sending an anonymous email, in case it led the hunters to her. She'd only been in Kotoyeesinay for a day, and already she'd miss the proper Mr. Maxen, the warm-hearted Aurelio at the diner, and especially the red-hot, handsome... her ankle twisted, and suddenly, as if she'd conjured him, she was tumbling into Chance McKennie's arms.

"Easy," he murmured, as he helped her stay upright. The

man smelled divine, like a combination of exotic spices, something civet-like, and earthy male. She blushed to realize she'd been sniffing him. Her nipples hardened as she barely controlled a shiver of desire. She had a momentary image of him nibbling on her neck, and her arching into him with uncontrollable passion.

She pushed herself away from him hastily, before she did something stupid, like kiss him. Her intense response to him was very unlike her.

She seriously needed to have her head examined.

## 4

C hance had never smelled anything so utterly perfect in his entire life as the woman in his arms. He would have liked to spend more time savoring the complex flavors of her scent, but she was pushing away, flustered, and his beast was roaring in his mind, surging to take form, right there in broad daylight. He stepped back as he clamped down on his jaw and concentrated on human thoughts. Driving his truck in rush-hour traffic. Marking a frame for a door hinge. Reading an architectural drawing. Kissing the woman in front of him. *Not helping!*

The subtle caress of her magic gave rise to an unsubtle hardening in his pants. Thankfully, his loose T-shirt covered the growing bulge that his jeans wouldn't hide for long. Just in case, he raised his arm so his sack of groceries covered his awakening desire.

"Sorry," she said. "Are you okay?"

"Yes," he replied, trying to smile. Wonder and delight bloomed with the realization that this gorgeous, sunny, *trés* sexy, fragile human woman was his beast's choice for a mate.

Terror and dismay took over as he realized the countless ways he could screw it up.

"I stepped on your foot, didn't I?" Remorse tinged her voice. "I'm so sorry. I'm a menace."

If he was like every other male shifter he'd known who'd just stumbled across his mate, he undoubtedly looked like a thunderstruck goofball. "I'm, uh, fine."

His beast clamored at him to pay attention to his mate, not his own worries. Beyond her mesmerizing eyes and full lips that he wanted to explore with his own, she looked pale and tired. The scent of feminine desire bloomed with her magic, and he could almost see it reaching for him. He trembled with the need to take her into his arms and find the nearest cave to join body and spirit with her, but that was out of the question. Not until she knew exactly what she was getting into, which meant first telling her the truth of who he was and not scaring the life out of her in the process. Not to mention finding someone to teach her how to use her magic, showing her who else really lived in Kotoyeesinay, and dealing with whatever had her needing sanctuary so badly that the elven magic had drawn her to town. It was just his luck to find the most difficult road possible to happiness with his destined mate.

"I wasn't watching, either, so it was my fault as much as yours." He made himself step back, in case he was crowding her, and gave her a more genuine smile. "Let's take each other to dinner to make amends." His beast snorted disdainfully at the cheesy pickup line. *Shut up,* he told the beast. *It's better than leaving a gift of a dead snake at her doorstep.*

She raised her eyebrows, then winced and frowned. Finally, she shook her head and laughed, throwing off whatever she'd been thinking. "I'm a hot mess right now, but

I'm too hungry to turn you down." She wiped away a sheen of perspiration from her forehead as she smoothed her hair. "Could we go back to the Blue Fairy? I'd like to thank Aurelio for all his help. The food smelled really good, and tonight, I actually have money." She patted her chest pocket, which drew his attention to her lushly rounded breasts. His mouth watered.

"Sounds good." He pointed toward the street. "Let's take my truck. It'll save me from having to come back for it later." She looked dead on her feet, and besides, he didn't want to share her with the other pedestrians, even if it was just for a few blocks. He glanced down the alleyway behind them. "Did you get the job at Turn of the Cards?"

"Yes." She frowned. "Mr. Maxen has no idea about money, though. He tried to pay me way too much."

"That's a nice problem to have," he teased, hoping to coax another smile from her.

She turned away to look at a display window. "Not as nice as you'd think."

Clearly, he needed to have a talk with Iolo Maxen to find out what that was about, but it could wait.

He walked around the front of the truck to unlock and open the passenger door for her. She slid her backpack off and dropped it and her hoodie at her feet as she climbed in. Her scent made his chest and neck flush. He closed her door gently, then walked quickly around and let himself in so he could start the engine and turn on the air conditioning. The cab was hot from the summer sun, but its small area meant it cooled quickly.

As he drove, he caught fleeting expressions of worry on her face when she thought he wasn't looking. He couldn't think of anything else to do but feed her and hope she'd tell him what was bothering her.

At the diner, Aurelio steered them to a small, two-person booth toward the back and told him their meals were on the house because Chance had helped the night before. Moira protested that she hadn't done anything, and she'd wanted to repay Aurelio's kindness, but he wouldn't hear of it.

"That was the best trout I've ever had." She pushed her plate away. "How was your Carnivore's Delight pizza?"

"Good." He'd never ordered off the tourist menu before, but Su Yen was a true genius in the kitchen.

Chance was glad Moira didn't suffer from the odd human female affliction of trying to impress him with how little she ate. She'd ordered a full dinner and cleaned her plate, and enjoyed the surprise delivery of lemon meringue pie with obvious relish. Her little moans of pleasure went straight to his groin, leaving him hard and aching in jeans that had become too tight from the moment they sat down and he'd gotten a nose full of her delectable scent. The essence of her called to his blood.

Moira looked more relaxed than she'd been before, but her right eye blinked a little too often, like something irritated it. He noticed that it happened whenever her subtle magic flared, and it belatedly occurred to him that her magic was fighting the town spells and charms that hid the true world of magic from her. No wonder his woman was exhausted. Except she wasn't his, yet.

"Do you believe in magic?" he asked as casually as he could, before he lost his nerve.

"Like the song? The one that was playing when we walked in?" She smiled, then looked thoughtful. "I don't believe in the woo-woo stuff like the town pushes, or like Mr. Maxen's customers talk about. But I believe in mundane magic. The smell of bacon, or the design of a spider web, or meeting someone you connect with right away, as if you've always known them, you just forgot for a moment." She blushed and looked away, then met his gaze again with a vulnerable, hopeful look. "I feel like that with you. I know it sounds crazy. I promise I'm not a stalker."

He admired her bravery more than anything. He reached across the table to capture her fingers and give them a quick squeeze. "I feel that, too." She didn't know the half of it, but it gave him hope that he wasn't going there by himself. He gave her a teasing smile. "I *am* a stocker, though. Night shift."

She got the joke a heartbeat later and laughed. "You're a punny man." She folded her napkin into a neat rectangle and placed it on the table. "What about you? Do you believe in magic?"

His tactical error hit him hard. If he said he didn't, he'd be lying to his mate, and if he said he did, he'd be alienating her. "Some kinds," he temporized. "Uh, what time is it?"

"Eight thirty-five, according to the diner's clock. What time do you have to be at work?"

"Nine," he answered automatically. Except he didn't, because he'd resigned the night before, and had to be out of his apartment in two days. Great. Nothing impressed a woman like being both jobless and homeless.

"We'd better get going, then, so you aren't late." She stood and slipped her backpack onto her shoulders. He'd noticed she unconsciously touched it often, like a talisman.

They stopped by the counter to thank Aurelio, then headed toward his truck. He couldn't resist slipping his hand into hers as they walked. She smiled and squeezed his fingers. "Thanks for dinner and driving."

"My pleasure." He let her into the truck, then got in and started it. "Back to Tinsel's?"

"Yes, please." She stuffed her hoodie into her backpack,

then wrapped her arms around it in her lap and rested her chin on it as he pulled into traffic, or what passed for it in Kotoyeesinay. She looked forlorn.

His simple-minded beast ordered him to find and kill whatever was making their mate unhappy. "Maybe it's none of my business, but is something wrong?"

She straightened up for a moment and smoothed her expression, then seemed to give up the pretense and slumped again. "I really like you, and I don't want to scare you away or anything, but my life is, well, complicated." She sighed and looked down at her backpack. "This crazy man named Witzer has been after me for three years. Not just cyberstalking, but actually sending people to take me to him. He's obsessed. He found me reading tarot cards at a Renaissance fair, and wants me to use my supposed 'magical gifts' to find out secrets about his enemies and predict the future for his business deals. I keep moving, cutting all ties, but he keeps finding me." Her arms tightened around her backpack. "This past winter, I thought I'd finally lost him for good, but six days ago, he found me, and I had to run again. He's willing to hurt people to get to me. Last year, they kidnapped and beat up the woman I shared a hostel room with in Vancouver. The news said it was 'drunk frat boys,' and the woman got a big settlement, but I think it was Witzer's goons, mistaking her for me."

Chance took a deep, centering breath, trying to calm the growling beast in his head. "That's why you take your backpack everywhere. It's your 'go' bag. That's why you need your car up and running."

She nodded, a look of relief crossing her face. Ordinary folks probably found her story hard to believe, but magical people knew that kind of trouble all too well. "He's textbook obsessive-compulsive, but he's old money and buy-his-own-country rich, and the police think I'm the one who's delusional. I think if he actually gets his hands on me, I'll never be free again." She shifted in her seat. "Luckily for me, I used my biological mother's name at the Ren fair, because it would have embarrassed my foster father to have his engineer coworkers find out about my summer job as a pretend fortune teller. Witzer doesn't know my legal name, so he never figured out where my foster parents live, or he'd have used them as leverage." She fidgeted with one of the backpack's zipper pulls. "It's not the life I would have chosen, but it hasn't been horrible up till now."

He glanced at her. "What changed?" He was suddenly uneasy about her answer, afraid she meant her attraction to him, but he needed to hear it.

She was silent for so long that his shoulder muscles started cramping from the tension. "I think something's wrong with my head." Her voice was small and scared.

"What makes you think so?" He hoped he sounded supportive, rather than terrified at the thought his mate could be dying before he had time to fall in love with her.

"I keep seeing flashes out of the corner of my eyes, like something's coming at me, or flickering just out of view, but there's nothing there. It started last night when we left the diner, but it's gotten progressively worse. Today in the store, I kept seeing... impossible things. Mostly in the mirrors. A talking bear with a Russian accent. A vampire, right out of a romance novel. A pair of young ravens instead of boys. Even Mr. Maxen, looking like a Tolkien elf, like the movies, only charcoal gray and prettier. A nineteenth-century oil painting that kept slowly changing. And when I ran into you tonight, you had amber eyes like a..." She trailed off, then shook her head. "I've always had a lively imagination, but even when I was little, I could always tell the difference between things I made up and the real world." She closed her eyes and rubbed her temples. "If I have a tumor or something, it could be pushing on parts of my brain, making me hallucinate. I don't have money or insurance. I can't even afford to get tested, much less treated."

She didn't smell sick, and his nose was superb at detecting such things. He suspected her innate magic was working around her learned skepticism and eroding the effect of the elven charms. They were never meant to hide anything from magical people.

His human relief warred with his beast's howling at her tangible despair. It was a wonder he could hear himself think. With shaky hands, he pulled the truck into the first available parking space on the side of the street, but left the engine running for the air conditioning. "Could I hold you for a minute?"

She looked up at him and sighed. "I'd like that."

He slid out from under the steering wheel toward her and opened his arms. She dropped her backpack to slump into his embrace, and he wrapped himself around her. His T-shirt dampened with her silent tears and warm breath. The feel of her, the smell of her, swamped his human thoughts. It was all he could do to stop his beast from voicing its purring pleasure at finally holding their mate.

"Sorry about your shirt," she mumbled.

He suspected no one had held her in a long time. "You can always cry with me." He rocked her slowly. She was strong and soft and fit perfectly in his arms.

She snuggled in closer and he stroked her hair. She needed someone much better with people and with words, someone who knew how to ease her into understanding, but right now, he was all she had.

"Was this Witzer guy your boyfriend?" That was his possessive beast asking.

A shudder went through her. "Hell, no. He's got twin sons older than me, and he's a major creeper." He did his best to hide his relief as she detailed the man's bizarre job offer and escalating salary and benefits offers, and the subsequent pursuit all over the country. "I take jobs for cash and make random choices on where to move next, but I think he has a security company tracking me, and eventually, they will find me. I'm probably just paranoid, but I think he wants to own me, like an expensive car, or an exotic pet."

"You're not paranoid," he murmured, "you're smart." The man sounded like a collector. Scary cautionary tales about collectors were a part of non-human lore the world over. Fortunately, most collectors knew better than to come anywhere near Kotoyeesinay, unless they had a death wish. Too many of the founding elves, fairies, witches, and shifters had unhappy personal history with them.

He wanted to pull her into his lap, but he didn't want her to discover how much she aroused him. She wasn't ready for that, even though he could smell the undercurrent of desire from her, too. "Maybe you really do have magic, just not the kind Witzer thinks. Maybe your magic told you what he really wants, and is what has kept you one step ahead of him for three years."

She gave a shaky laugh. "That would be fitting justice." She gave his chest a pat, then straightened up to give him a searching look. "You really believe that, don't you?"

After a moment, he nodded. "I do." He had a hard enough road to be with his mate as it was, without lying to her. He'd seen other shifters lose human mates over less. "I think it's like a sixth sense, one you didn't know you had. It's been operating without you knowing, and now you have to learn to use it, so it works when you want it to."

She smiled wistfully. "I'd have loved to have heard that when I was twelve." After a moment, she shook her head minutely. "It's a nice thought, but—"

A loud thump of something hitting the passenger door startled them both.

Moira looked out the window. "Huh. Not something you often see in the summer."

When he leaned closer to look, he saw Tinsel's red-and-gold sleigh—the one he'd built and painted—resting against the truck's passenger door.

"What does it look like to you?" he asked cautiously, not sure what the sleigh's protective illusion spell would show her.

"An old-fashioned miniature sleigh, with ice runners and everything. Looks like the one I saw on Tinsel's porch. I thought it was just decoration." She turned to him. "I'll call her and ask if hers is missing." She pulled out her cellphone.

He hid a sigh, knowing his what-are-the-odds luck was flaring again. "If she'd like, we can take it back in my truck."

Moira pulled out a card from her chest pocket, then held it out to him. "Tinsel gave me her number and yours, but she didn't mark which was which."

"The bottom one's mine." Tinsel's matchmaker streak had often annoyed him, but if it prompted Moira to call him, he'd send Tinsel a rum-soaked fruitcake every year on that date.

He would have unashamedly used his superior hearing to listen to both sides of the conversation, but he didn't have to because she put it on her phone's tinny speaker. It seemed a certain group of miscreant wolf boys had attempted a joy ride, only to have the sleigh dump them in the neighbor's swimming pool, then fly off down the street.

"*The sleigh went looking for someone it could trust,*" explained Tinsel.

"Er, lucky it found us, then," said Moira. Her indulgent smile said she was humoring an old woman's fancy. "We'll bring it right now, so Chance isn't late for work."

Tinsel thanked them and disconnected.

Chance approached the sleigh cautiously, in case its defensive magic thought he was another thief, but fortunately, it docilely allowed him to pull it back from Moira's door so she could get out. It took both of them to lift the bulky sleigh into the bed of his truck. The illusion spell made her see wheels where there were none, but didn't hide the tingle from the magic that ran it. She attributed it to a minor short in the non-existent electrics.

"I take it," she said, wiping her hands on her jeans, "that the Wolf boys are known troublemakers in this town." She laughed. "Their parents must be on everyone's speed dial."

He didn't correct her impression that it was just one family named Wolf. The local population of wolf shifters thrived in Kotoyeesinay, so it could have been the pups from one or more of a dozen different families. It was more a sin of omission, but he felt as guilty as if he'd lied to her.

At Tinsel's, Moira helped him carry the sleigh up to the porch. She was even stronger than she looked, which had both him and his beast purring inside. Especially when she explained she'd gotten a lot of exercise working on a dairy farm. His beast liked steak.

He was getting used to her subtle magic that sparked at odd moments, but he couldn't tell what it was doing, other than fighting to be free of the town illusions. A witch might be able to figure it out, but he didn't know very many people in town, owing to his loner nature, so he didn't know who to ask, or more importantly, who Moira would believe. It occurred to him that Iolo Maxen at Turn of the Cards was a unique *dywylled* elf who could handle any metal, loved technology, and specialized in repairing magical devices. Chance had done some fine woodwork repair on a magical spice cabinet, and liked him. Since she already knew Iolo, maybe the old elf could figure out what Moira's magic was and help ease her into the truth.

He ignored his beast's demand to scoop her into his arms and ravish her on the porch swing, and settled for politely slipping his hand into hers. His beast chuffed in vindication when she immediately drew him into a full-press embrace. He didn't even try to stop himself from meeting her upturned face halfway and kissing her like she was the only woman on earth. To him, she was.

Their tongues twined like soft, questing vines, sending his heart thumping and the sound of hers racing. Her little moan of pleasure went straight to his groin and hardened him in seconds. He sternly reminded himself that humans liked things slow, and started to angle his hips away, but she grabbed his ass with both hands and pulled him tightly against her muscular stomach. "I like knowing you want me as much as I want you," she breathed, nibbling along his jawline and down his neck.

"How could I not?" he asked, skimming his hands down her back to memorize the feel of her curves. "You're perfect." He nuzzled behind her ear to fill his nose with her unique and addicting scent, as complex as curry, with hints of cream, cardamom, and melting snow.

A distant chime sounded more than once. It took a moment for him to identify it as the huge grandfather clock inside the entryway of Tinsel's home.

"Oh, hell, my timing sucks." Moira pulled back to look up at him. "I've made you late for work."

He started to deny it, but then he'd have to explain that he didn't have a job anymore, and then he'd have to explain *why* he didn't have a job, and then... he swallowed. "I'll, uhm, be okay. I'll make up the time tomorrow."

The only thing that made it possible for him to release her was that she looked just as reluctant to let go of him. He unashamedly adjusted his pants to ease his rock-hard dick into a more comfortable position. She gave him a sultry smile and smoothed her blouse, revealing the firmly pointed tips of her nipples, visible even through her bra. He swallowed again.

"Could we see each other again tomorrow?" she asked. Her tone was casual, but her expression was a mix of longing and trepidation. Her bravery humbled the man in him, and made his beast confident she'd be an excellent defender of his cubs.

"Yes," he said firmly, giving her no reason to doubt him. "I'll come find you after work."

She smiled wider. "I get off at–"

The front door opened, revealing a beaming Tinsel. "Oh good, you got Blitzen back to his proper home." She pointed to the sleigh. "Those wolf boys better be careful what they wish for in the next few months. I'll be adding security... " She peered up at him, then looked at Moira. "Oh, did I interrupt something delightfully steamy?" She waggled her eyebrows suggestively at them both. "Carry on, then." She shut the door.

Moira laughed out loud. "Everyone in this town is crazy."

"Ah-hem." Chance cleared his throat loudly and gave her a mock affronted look.

"Yes, you're crazy, too, and so am I." She waved toward the street. "Go to work, or I'll drag you upstairs to the Lost Princess bedroom so you can find me, and then you'll really be late for work, and your boss will fire you."

He gave her a mock salute. "Tomorrow," he promised, then turned and walked briskly away, before he followed her in like a hungry stray.

It had been too long since he'd let his beast out, and now, he was paying the price with his lack of control. His beast didn't like civilization or daylight, so tonight after it cooled off, he would visit the familiar peaks and let his beast run and hunt for a while, to get it out of his system. He'd start telling Moira the truth tomorrow.

## 5

Moira had taken Mr. Maxen at his word about her casual wardrobe, but she brought her only sweater just in case it made her look slightly more professional. Pandora found it in the open backpack within thirty minutes and brazenly made it into a nest.

Though the business and Mr. Maxen seemed as old as some of the small antiques he sold, his computer-networked cash-register system was state-of-the-art, and even allowed him to offer free Wi-Fi to his customers. Maybe she could use it after the store closed to catch up on her emails. Not that she'd have many, since she couldn't keep any friends. She used secure, anonymizing software and changed accounts and providers often, so she wouldn't be traceable by Witzer's snoops. At least it kept the spam down.

Fortunately, the morning wasn't as busy as the day before, which gave Mr. Maxen time to teach her how to record sales, handle refunds, and enter special orders. In between customers and lessons, she kept Pandora out of trouble and familiarized herself with the store's eclectic merchandise. She'd always had a fondness for mirrors, and practically every display had one, some jaw-droppingly expensive.

As long as she stayed out front where it was bright and cheery, the peripheral vision flashes were minimal. The moment she got close to the hieroglyph-decorated doorway that led to the back area, the motion-activated lights came on, and her vision flickered like she was at a rock concert.

In idle moments, she found herself thinking of increasingly outlandish strategies to run into Chance sooner than after work. He was not only hotter than high noon, he was the nicest man she'd ever run into, literally or figuratively. No ordinary man would let a woman he'd just met cry on his shoulder about her insane life, and actually believe her wild story, then make out with her on Tinsel's porch. Her dreams of him last night had left her drenched with unquenched need that she'd had to take care of in the shower. It was probably just as well she didn't know where he lived, or she'd be stalking him on her lunch hour.

A few minutes after eleven, Mr. Maxen handed her a square wooden cube carved with floral decorations that turned out to be made of tiny Nordic runes. "Please make a place for this in the antiques cabinet by the door. Then I'll send you for lunch. Where would you like to go?"

The box felt old and warm to her, like it had been sitting in a sunny window. She rubbed her thumb over it, admiring the hand-tooled workmanship. "I've only been to one restaurant, so I'm no help. You choose. I'll eat anything." She looked at the bottom of the box as she opened the cabinet, hoping to see the initials of whoever made it, but it was covered in runes, too. She traced almost invisible lines and realized what it was. "This puzzle box is beautiful."

Mr. Maxen gave her a sharp smile. "What else do you think it is?"

He'd been doing that all morning, asking her to guess what things were for, and correcting her when she got them wrong. She'd been nervous at first, trying to be serious and remember everything, but he'd made it seem like a fun game, and encouraged her whimsical imagination. "Storing secrets, of course," she said breezily. "The kind you're dying to tell, but can't trust anyone with, so you lock them in the stalwart heart of the box. The runes make the box indestructible."

Mr. Maxen laughed. "You have a telling gift." He pulled out a folder with a collection of menus. "It was originally meant to hold keys. They were bigger back when the box was made."

"Oh, like the fake rocks for hiding a spare door key? Sweet." She opened the glass-paned doors, then gave the box a place of honor on the shelf, nudging aside a stand with a fussy hanging glass chime that seemed to quiver with the slightest breeze. She decided its job was to announce the presence of people with bad intentions, like shoplifters. The gorgeously detailed miniature cheval mirror on the right was for seeing the unseen, like ghosts… or better yet, seeing someone's true nature. Its small size made it seem harmless and belied the true strength of its magic. She laughed at herself. Maybe she should take up storytelling for a museum.

She closed the cabinet door gently, then went back to the counter, where Mr. Maxen handed her the menu he'd selected. "I'll take the vegetarian pot pie and a large milk. Order whatever you want, and tell them to put it on my tab." He handed her the phone. "In the meantime, I'll find the fluffy monster and feed her, too." He went through the beaded curtain toward the back.

Moira had indulged herself at Tinsel's huge breakfast

buffet that morning, so she called in Mr. Maxen's order and a simple sandwich and iced tea for herself. Outside of hauling a few boxes, her new job wasn't nearly as physically taxing as mucking out stables. She felt a pang for her lost friendships. She even missed the dairy cows, who'd had surprisingly varied personalities and liked being cleaned and brushed.

She was making new friends in Kotoyeesinay, and knew she'd soon have to leave them, too. She'd lost too much time between Nunn and Kotoyeesinay. Witzer wouldn't leave her alone now, not after coming so close to catching her again. It wasn't fair to bring his violently delusional brand of crazy down on the gentle crazy that was Kotoyeesinay.

"Why the long face, Ms. Graham?" asked Mr. Maxen.

Moira straightened up and pasted a smile on her face. "Just a sad thought, sir. I'm sure the walk to the restaurant will banish it." She slid her backpack on her shoulders.

Mr. Maxen raised an eyebrow, but thankfully, he didn't pry. She wouldn't have liked to lie to him, but the less he knew, the safer he'd be if Witzer's a-hole team ever questioned him. She'd learned that lesson the hard way, after what happened to that poor woman in Vancouver the day after Moira had left.

Despite the high altitude and relatively northern latitude, the heat of the noonday sun had the locals complaining about a heat wave and Moira going out of her way to stick to the shaded areas on the way back from the restaurant.

The walk took her by Knight's Garage, where poor Frankie languished in the back lot. The owner, Shepherd, confirmed her suspicion that the engine was toast, but quoted her a surprisingly reasonable price for a rebuilt engine to replace it. Apparently, he had one taking up room in storage that he hadn't been able to use for anything else, but with a little effort, would fit the Frankencar. If she hoarded her funds, she'd be able to pay for everything within the week. It made her uncomfortable not to be able to pay Tinsel, too, but her temporary hostess had adamantly refused any money for either the bed or the breakfast, and wouldn't even let her move to a smaller room in the castle. Moira needed to think of something she could do for Tinsel in trade before leaving.

She ought to be relieved that she could soon move on, to stay ahead of Witzer, but all it did was depress her. The thought of having to leave kind, sexy Chance McKennie before she even got to know him made her shoulders slump. Life on the run was truly the pits.

Before she knew it, she was back on Wizard Street. She gave herself a shake. Wallowing in her sorrows didn't help anything, and it made her inattentive, which she couldn't afford. She threw her shoulders back and marched herself into Turn of the Cards.

She couldn't help but smile when she saw Chance standing at the counter, talking earnestly with Mr. Maxen. She resisted the temptation to saunter up beside Chance and caress the back pocket of his jeans, which just happened to be covering his beautifully muscular butt. She suspected Mr. Maxen wouldn't approve.

She didn't know if she'd approve, either. She wasn't the sexually aggressive type, but something about Chance made her want to throw off her usual reserve and pounce. Maybe she was a sucker for chiseled men with wavy red hair.

"Lunch," she announced as she set the bag on the counter. "What are you two conspiring about?"

Chance smiled like he was happily surprised to see her, which was odd, because he knew she worked there. "We were just discussing a mutual interest."

"Really?" She set the drink tray on the counter and pulled out the straws. "What?"

They exchanged a glance. Mr. Maxen reached into the bag. "I'm hiring Mr. McKennie to renovate the upstairs area into a livable space. He's agreed to move in here starting the day after tomorrow while he works."

Chance's eyes widened momentarily, giving her the impression that at least part of that was news to him. "Uhm, yes, the general store let me go, so I have some free time."

The implication of his words sunk in. "Oh no, I got you fired, didn't I?" She shouldn't have given into the overwhelming temptation to kiss him last night and make him late. "I'm so sorry."

Chance put his hand over hers. "It wasn't your fault. I resigned."

"You did?" It was hard to ignore his touch, but she had to know she wasn't messing up his life. "Why?"

Chance sighed. "Because I was tired of not using my skills. Working the night shift meant I never saw anyone. It was sheer luck I met you." His soft smile melted her heart, and made her want to kiss him senseless, right then and there.

Mr. Maxen cleared his throat loudly. "And it's my good fortune to be able to make use of Mr. McKennie's expertise."

Moira groped to find her rational thoughts again. She took out her sandwich and showed it to Chance. "Tuna salad. Want half?"

His crooked smile made him even sexier than his jeans did. "No, I just ate breakfast." He was obviously still on a night-shift schedule. Left to her own devices, she was a night owl, herself.

An idea struck. "Mr. Maxen, I'd like to earn some of that outrageous salary you're paying me by helping with the renovation. I'm pretty handy with power tools, and I have experience."

"You do?" He looked shocked.

She tried not to take his skeptical tone personally. Old-fashioned Mr. Maxen probably wasn't used to women who knew basic carpentry. "Sure. I can frame and drywall, and tape seams like a pro. I'm pretty good with a paint roller, too, at least for prime coats."

Unexpectedly, Chance came to her aid. "The project will go a lot faster with her help." His confidence in her made her want to kiss him again. She was beginning to think pretty much anything he did would make her want to kiss him. *Later,* she promised herself.

"I can work evenings, after we close the store. Besides, it'll be cooler." She waved toward the ceiling. "Are you wanting to keep the original bedrooms as they are?"

"I hadn't decided." He gave both her and Chance a considering glance. "Why don't I close the shop for a few minutes and we go up and look?"

The afternoon alternately flew and dragged by, depending on whether she was helping customers or counting the minutes until they could get started working on remodeling the second floor. She loved projects like this, and learning new skills.

The upstairs originally had four bedrooms plus a bathroom, but some previous owner had combined a couple of the bedrooms by the simple expedient of knocking down a wall. Mr. Maxen had lived up there when he'd first bought the store about twenty-five years ago, but found it too hot in the summer and too cold in the winter. He bought a separate small home and used the store's second floor for seasonal retail stock and old furniture.

His goal was to renovate the rooms so he could host occasional out-of-town guests, rather than send them to the expensive casino or tiny motel. The new space would have two airy bedrooms with big closets, and a central sitting room with a small bar area to take advantage of the original woodwork near the stairs. Chance would work with a plumber to enlarge and modernize the bathroom, and add a small, private powder room to the larger of the two bedrooms. He'd sketched the plans as they talked, and Mr. Maxen approved.

While she helped customers, Chance was making detailed measurements and evaluating the house's plumbing, electrical, and heating systems to see what needed upgrading. It was just as well she had to work to keep her busy, because every overhead thump she heard reminded her he was there, and fueled her erotic fantasies of what she could be doing with a hot handyman. He'd have never gotten anything done.

Right at seven, Mr. Maxen invited her and Chance to the small office area, handed her a cream-colored envelope with her day's pay, then announced he was leaving immediately. "I want to get an early start on my day off."

She'd forgotten the store was closed on Mondays. "Could Chance and I still work upstairs tonight and tomorrow? It'd be a good time for the noisy demolition work." She glanced at Chance to see if he concurred.

He nodded. "Shepherd Knight said he'd lend me some

demolition tools, and has a roll-off debris bin we can use. He's dropping them and the I-beam off later tonight."

Mr. Maxen frowned. "Pandora and I are leaving for a dem... er, Laramie this evening."

Moira started to say the project could wait, but it couldn't. As soon as her car was ready, she had to make another random jump, and fast. She owed it to both Mr. Maxen and Chance to do as much as she could before she left. "Would you trust Chance or me with the keys and the alarm codes?"

A lucky car headlight flashed high across the mirror next to the stairs.

Mr. Maxen held up his hands in surrender. "No need to use your magic, Ms. Graham. I accept your generous offer. I'll even throw in dinner wherever you like. Have them put it on my tab."

"My magic?" Everyone in Kotoyeesinay seemed to have magic on the brain.

Mr. Maxen glanced at Chance, then gave her a wry smile. "Your power of persuasion."

She was certain that wasn't what he'd meant, but she didn't want to argue with her boss.

He showed them how to work the alarm and had them memorize the eight-digit code and write down his phone number in case of trouble. He showed Chance the silent alarm switch under the sales counter that would alert the sheriff's office. "Oh, and one more thing. You should both stay out of the workroom area as much as possible while I'm not there."

Chance nodded, but he was busy reviewing a list he'd pulled out of his work vest pocket.

"Don't worry about that," she said firmly. "The lights in there give me a nasty headache."

He tilted his head inquisitively. "They're the same out here." He pointed up toward the fluorescent ceiling fixtures. "These don't bother you?"

She shrugged one shoulder and looked down. "Sometimes the reflections off the mirrors do, especially the big ones."

"Don't forget to lock up when you leave." He shouldered the soft carrier that contained a wiggly white kitten, then handed her the spare key. "Perhaps you should quit trying so hard not to see what's in front of you."

That clinched it. Everyone in the town of Kotoyeesinay was crazy. But she didn't care, because after Mr. Maxen left, she had a whole evening with the man she'd been dreaming about day and night. It would hurt like fire to let him go, but if life on the run had taught her nothing else, it was to seize the moment, because it would never come again.

## 6

Chance knew his plan to talk to Moira about her magic and the people in Kotoyeesinay was doomed from the moment he saw Moira realize they'd be alone together for the evening. The resulting gleam in her eye made his beast thrum with pleasure and his body redirect most of the blood his brain needed for thinking to his groin.

He temporarily distracted them both by ordering food, and making a list of the supplies they'd need for the renovation while they ate dinner in the little office area. Iolo told them to make use of the accounts he had with practically every other business in town, but neither Chance nor Moira wanted to buy anything major without Iolo approving it first.

Moira grabbed her backpack. "I want to change into a T-shirt. Let's go up and figure out logistics." Her swaying rear mesmerized him as she climbed the stairs, so much so that he nearly ran into her when she stopped at the top.

"Oh, shoot," she said. "I forgot to ask Mr. Maxen what to

do about all his stuff. It'll get filthy if we don't move it, or at least cover it."

"Shepherd is using his big truck to bring the new header beam for the ceiling, and I asked him to bring some extra tarps. He'll be here about eight." To keep from touching her, he busied himself by taking off his work vest and hanging it on the newel post. "Meanwhile, we can corral everything in the southeast bedroom."

"Sounds good." She gave him a sassy smile as she fished a faded iron-gray T-shirt out of her backpack. "I can add 'herding furniture' to my résumé."

As they carried dressers, trunks, small tables, and chairs, they talked about what to do next. The heating and air-conditioning systems were both good, so all they'd need was new ducting and improved insulation all around to solve the temperature problem. Heated baseboards and upgrading the windowpanes would help in deep winter. The new floorplan would also reinstate the load-bearing wall the previous owner had compromised by combining bedrooms.

They decided to put any reusable wood in with the furniture. She had a notion much like his about creating a temporary chute out of tarp and a rough frame so they could simply drop the discards from the window of the northeast bedroom and have it land in the roll-off.

After forty minutes, the furniture and boxes were stacked, and they were both sweating rivers in the second-floor's stuffy heat.

Night had fallen outside, but the waning moon would give Chance plenty of light to see by, if he borrowed his beast's vision without actually shifting. Selective shifting was an alpha trick his magical cougar mother had taught him. She could have been alpha of the cougar pride, but she chose happiness with her mate and child instead of the difficult task of dragging the hidebound, chauvinistic pride into the twenty-first century. The local wolf pack, ancient enemy of the pride, was no more enlightened and even more bigoted, which was why his father resigned his hard-earned beta position to make a home with his mate. Chance had grown up in the security of their deep and abiding love. He wanted that for his own children. For himself.

Moira fanned herself by pulling the hem of her T-shirt up and down, giving him tantalizing glimpses of her rounded but muscled stomach. "Do you think we could open the windows for some ventilation?"

"Good idea." Her natural scent, magnified by her perspiration, was making it hard to think of anything beyond kissing her all over.

He turned to the window, flipped the levers, and pulled up on the sash. It stuck for a moment, then opened. He felt a flare of the building's wards through his fingers and hoped he hadn't just sent a silent alarm to the sheriff's station or the ogre-run security company. Iolo had cleverly keyed the building's wards to both Chance and Moira, under the guise of teaching them to use the mundane security system, but for obvious reasons, hadn't explained them.

He turned back to her just in time to catch her wince.

"Damn," she muttered, rubbing her temple. "I thought I was getting better."

He needed to tell her what was happening, but the words stuck in this throat. He wasn't usually a coward, but he could lose his mate if he handled it wrong. He pulled out one of the chairs and pointed to it. "Rest here a minute." She sat and closed her eyes, toeing off her loosely tied sneakers and her socks.

He studied her a long moment to make sure she was okay, then turned off the overhead light and left her there so he could go open the rest of the second-floor windows. As he forced open one paint-glued window after another, he racked his brain for how to start a conversation he knew wasn't going to go well. For all her ready sense of humor and imagination, underneath, she was inherently practical and conditioned to be deeply skeptical. He'd bet that as a child, she'd been told to quit dreaming, quit making things up, quit lying about things only she could see. She'd need proof, and despite his potential gifts, the only magic he could reliably work involved shifting into an eight-hundred-pound beast that wanted to groom her and get a good ear rub in return. But he had to do something, because she was suffering needlessly. He stepped into the darkened bedroom.

"Moira, we need to talk..." His tongue cleaved to the roof of his mouth. She stood by the window, smiling, eyes closed, lit only by moonlight. Her T-shirt trailed on the floor from her hand, leaving her wearing only her thin bra and jeans.

She turned to look at him, making no move to cover herself. Her slow smile said she enjoyed the stunning effect she had on him. Her curling finger invited him in.

His beast surged. He knew his eyes probably flashed amber as he stripped off his T-shirt and took three long strides to close the distance between them. He crushed her to his chest, craving the feel of her skin on his. He plundered her mouth, reveling in the sexiest woman he'd ever tasted. She gave as good as she got, voicing a low moan that almost sounded like a purr. He ground himself into her, drowning the pain of the suddenly too-tight pants with the pleasure of feeling her on him. He came up for air, only to have the scent of her blossoming desire drive him mad.

He slid a hand up her side to cup her lush, pillowy breast and brush his thumb over her stiff nipple. Even through the fabric of her bra, the tip was diamond hard. She arched into his touch. "Yes, Chance, yes."

Jealous of the moonlight and whoever else might be flying by, he pivoted her in a wide circle that took them near the newel post of the four-post bed. She glanced at the bed, which they'd covered with stacks of boxes and plastic tubs. "Bad planning. We'll have to improvise."

She pushed his chest, and he reluctantly moved back, closing his eyes in case his beast was visible. He opened them immediately when she took his hand and placed it on her bare breast, her bra nowhere to be seen. "Kiss me here."

She raised her hands to grab onto the newel post above her, lifting her luscious breasts for him to feast on. He supported her back with one arm and enveloped her whole dark areola with his hungry mouth, sliding his tongue back and forth across her turgid nipple. Her little gasps of pleasure spurred him to cover her other breast with his free hand and scissor its nipple between his fingers. Her scent sharpened with desire as her hips began rhythmically grinding forward.

"Touch me," she breathed. "I burn for you."

His mating pheromones must already be affecting her. One more confirmation that he was hers, and she was his. His beast lunged forward again, and he closed his eyes. He wanted nothing more than to bury his aching, surging dick into the warm, moist heat of her core, and bathe her womb with life-giving seed, mating her for life, but he couldn't do it. Not until she knew what it meant. Not until he knew she would stay. But he could ease her immediate need, and his.

He dropped to his knees in front of her and swiftly unbuttoned her jeans, then wrenched them and her underwear to her knees. Almost before she kicked them off, he buried his face in her gloriously natural mons and inhaled the full scent of her, making him drunk on her pleasure. He used his shifter strength to lift her hips to his mouth and slid his tongue downward, brushing past her clit to lap up the wetness he found at her entrance. He circled back up to her hardened clit and flicked it several times with the tip of his tongue, backing off at the first warning spasm. He glanced up to see her head thrown back as she rolled one of her own nipples with her fingers. He repeated it twice more, wanting her first orgasm from him to be as good as he could make it, without the teasing becoming torture. The third time, he stayed at her clit and covered it with his tongue while sliding a finger into her entrance and up inside her slick walls. A couple more thrusts and flicks of his tongue sent her up and over the edge, clit and core spasming hard and strong for him. He hung on for the ride until she came down, dimly aware that she'd been murmuring his name the whole time.

He'd had sex with other women before, and made sure they enjoyed it, but nothing in the world compared to the soul-deep satisfaction of pleasuring his mate.

Moira looked down at the man kneeling between her legs. She should have been embarrassed. She was buck naked, hanging onto a heavy antique bedpost like a lifeline, and he was still in his jeans, his face and soft beard wet with her juices. But after the best damn orgasm she'd ever had, she couldn't be bothered with modesty.

She sank to her knees in front of him and rested her hands on his broad shoulders. "Hi, there."

He smiled. A reflection of moonlight turned his hazel eyes to golden amber, and she couldn't be bothered to care about that, either. She allowed her hands to drift downward to his slightly puffy nipples and brushed them, then licked both her thumbs and did it again, drawing a shudder from him. "I'd very much like to return the favor."

"You don't have to–" His eyes widened and his hips thrust forward when her hand landed on the iron bar in his pants.

She leaned forward to nuzzle his neck and gently nip at his earlobe, while languidly stroking him through his pants. "I want to." She undid the top button of his jeans and eased the zipper down. The damp fly of his boxers clung to the tip of his penis. "I need to."

He palmed her face and kissed her, still tasting of her and him commingled. "Yes."

He stood and removed his boots and socks, then dropped his pants and boxers. The moonlight made the sheen of perspiration and sparse red drift of hair across his chest and down his sculpted abdomen sparkle like white gold. His shaft stood so proud and erect she almost saluted it, but her mouth ached to taste him. She glided her hands up his fantastic thighs and encircled him. She pumped once, twice, then drew in a deep breath and took him into her mouth all at once, as far as she could go, sliding her tongue to caress the sensitive underside.

He growled in pleasure and caressed the side of her head, then pushed her braid to her back. "That feels..." He threw his head back with a gasp and grabbed the bedpost above when she cupped his balls. He widened his stance to give her better access.

The constant twitches of his hips said he was already close, and she wanted him to feel as good as she had. She suctioned her mouth tight around him and started moving up and down with purpose, circling her fingers around the base to steady him.

He was growling continuously now. She sped up to as fast as she could go, and slid one wet finger back behind his balls to rub his perineum, because it seemed like the right thing to do.

He snarled as his whole body tensed when his orgasm overtook him. She swallowed what she could and let the rest overflow down her chin and paint her breasts. She heard a crack overhead, and realized he'd broken the thick bedpost with the strength of his grip.

She delicately licked the sensitive head until she felt his tension subside.

She wiped her chin and stood, slightly unsteady, unexpectedly giddy that he'd enjoyed it so much. She hadn't had real sex with anyone in four years, and no one except the occasional book boyfriend to fantasize about. He sat on the edge of the bed and pulled her into a snuggling embrace on his lap that felt so right that she forgot the sweat and fluids that coat them both. "Now *that* was magic."

He chuckled. "No, that was just you and me." He kissed her temple. "Together."

She flattened her palm on the curve of his pectoral muscle. "So tell me what you think magic is, if not that?"

He stilled beneath her, but his heart sped up a little. "It's... complicated."

"Tell me. I won't laugh." She pulled back to look at his shadowed, serious face. "I don't promise to believe, but I won't laugh."

He shook his head.

She sighed. Mind-blowing sex brought the illusion of trust, but not the real thing. Her chest chilled, and she felt sticky. "Do you think Mr. Maxen would mind if I took a quick shower up here?" She slid off his warm thighs to stand on the wood floor. That soft lump next to the window looked like her T-shirt.

"Don't leave." He slid forward and spread his legs, then pulled her to face him in a loose embrace. He looked serious, and a bit worried. He started to speak, then let his breath out, as if he was having trouble finding the words. "The world is full of magic, and creatures that can use it. Elves, shifters, fairies, witches, demons, beings you've never heard of. They're all real." He tilted his head toward the window. "Some them live here in Kotoyeesinay. It's a centuries-old sanctuary created by a glade of golden elves, to protect themselves and others from the mundane world, where fearful humans would kill them and worse."

"Okay," she said. "I haven't seen anything like that, but I'll take your word for it."

He shook his head. "You *have* seen it. You told me in the truck last night. The vampire customer in the store. Iolo Maxen, the beautiful dark elf. Sergei, the Siberian bear shifter." He tilted his head toward the window again. "Powerful illusion charms and spells protect people in the town and make ordinary humans only see what they expect to see. You're not an ordinary human, but you believe you are. I think the flashes in your peripheral vision come from your magic fighting the spells, and your mind explaining away what you really see."

She couldn't doubt his sincerity. "I haven't felt any magic." She twitched an eyebrow and the corners of her mouth. "Except when you made me come with your tongue."

He smiled briefly. "You definitely have magic, and more than just your miraculous mouth on me." He gave her a quick kiss.

"Are you saying I'm a witch?" She didn't know if she liked that.

He shook his head. "Doesn't feel like it. Witches are flashy. Your magic is subtle, almost undetectable, but I'm sensitive to it."

"That means you're not an ordinary human, either."

"True," he agreed. His jaw tensed, but he held her gaze.

She braced herself to ask the obvious question. She was afraid she was falling for the startlingly handsome, naked man in front of her, and wanted to have her wicked way with him as often as she could before one of them had to leave, but she was suddenly afraid to find out how deep his fantasy ran. It wouldn't be right to take advantage of a man who needed professional help.

Three muffled chimes sounded.

"Shit." Chance moved her back and stood up. "That's my phone. Shepherd said he'd text me when he got here."

Her eyes widened. "Shit!" She bent to scoop up her pants and T-shirt and mentally added a dollar to her swear fund. Where was her damn bra?

He pulled on his pants, then tossed her bra to her. "You can get dressed in the bathroom. I'll stall him."

She grabbed her athletic shoes and socks. "My backpack." She'd been so distracted by acting on her sexual fantasies and Chance's belief in magic that she'd lost track of it. She couldn't afford mistakes like that. Cold reality was a ruthless wolf with sharp teeth.

He hopped around on one foot, pulling on a sock. "Near the stairs. I'll bring it to you."

She kicked his boot to him, from where it had somehow landed near the door. "Thanks." She wanted to kiss him, so he'd know she meant to thank him for more than just the backpack, but there wasn't time.

Luckily, the bathroom proved to have enough toilet paper for a hasty cleanup, and Chance thoughtfully gave her his big red bandanna to use as a washcloth. The slightly age-fogged mirror showed she looked only slightly ravished by the time she got her clothes back on and used her brush to flatten the wavy dark wisps around her hairline. She'd have liked to undo and re-braid her hair, but she heard loud boots clomping up the stairs. Chance was probably giving her as much warning as he could.

She stuffed Chance's damp bandanna in her front pocket, zipped up her backpack, flushed the toilet, and stepped into the hall, just in time to see Chance and Shepherd hit the top of the stairs. Chance carried a full stack of folded bright blue tarps, and Shepherd had an armful of white plastic pipes.

"Shepherd offered to help put together the trash drop." Chance smiled, and Shepherd blushed.

She beamed at them both. "The more the merrier. What can I do?"

Chance tilted his head toward the stairs. "Bring up the last two tarps and my tool bag from the office, and see if you can find the switch for the lights out back."

Bless the man for accepting her help and not relegating her to the sidelines. It was annoying to have to prove her capabilities time and time again. She put her backpack next to the bannister, then practically skipped down the stairs.

When she returned, she found the men at the window they'd be using for the chute's entrance.

"...thought about hanging the frame from here instead of nailing it to the outside," said Shepherd, tapping the window frame, "but I'm worried the wood won't hold."

Moira put the toolbox and tarps on the floor, then stepped closer to the window. "If you have any winch wire or furniture straps, you can do what we rigged after the hurricane. Put a folded blanket over this"—she patted the sill—"to protect it, and bolt the straps to the framing studs below. We have to replace the plaster anyway, because of the new ducting and insulation."

"That'll work," said Chance, crouching to rap on the wall with his knuckles. He smiled up at her, like he couldn't help it. She knew how he felt. Just seeing his thighs flex under his jeans as he stood up made her want to kiss him, then lead him back to the bedroom again.

"Now all we need is the lights." He pointed toward the window.

"Oh yeah. Lights. On it." She made herself leave the bedroom before she lost control altogether.

Shepherd's gravelly voice echoed after her. "Your mate is a clever woman."

"She's not my... here, hold this," said Chance.

Moira paused at the top of the stairs, hoping to hear more, but they stopped talking. She thought about the words as she went down the stairs. If "mate" was a slang term for "hookup," then she was glad Chance wasn't the type to lick and tell. She didn't even want to think about the implications if Shepherd meant "mate" like shifter romance novels used it.

She remembered seeing a bank of light switches near the loading dock, so she turned right at the foot of the stairs and headed through the wide doorway, into the cooler air and motion-activated lights of the workroom, still pondering her growing connection with Chance. He was definitely crazy-hot, and she wanted him again, soon, but he might also be crazy-crazy, and she wouldn't be able to live with herself if their relationship made him worse.

It wasn't until she got well past the entryway, into the

middle of the big room, that she remembered Mr. Maxen had told them to stay out. She froze, meaning to turn around, but was suddenly beset by flashes everywhere, as if dozens of paparazzi cameras flashed in her face. She slapped her hands over her eyes, and the flashes vanished. She counted to ten, then angled her hands away briefly. More flashes dazzled her before she blocked her eyes again.

She couldn't go forward or backward playing blind man's bluff without running into shelves full of irreplaceable antiques. From the thumping she heard above, neither Shepherd nor Chance would hear her if she called out for help.

Besides, it was too embarrassing. She'd just been feeling smug about being treated as an equal, and they'd start thinking she was fragile. She didn't want to be a sheltered princess in a tower, she wanted to be a self-rescuing princess who shot back at imperial stormtroopers and led the rebel alliance. Who stood up to evil, rather than running from it.

Chance had said the flashes were caused by her magic, trying to help her see the truth. She took a deep breath and let it out slowly. The secret truth that she'd hidden away for so long was, she *wanted* to see. Wanted to believe what Chance believed, and not just because she wanted him.

The idea of a hidden world—and acceptance for the rare, the unique, the impossible—filled her with a deep longing to be a part of it. She loved her foster parents dearly, but they'd never quite understood her. She'd always thought it was because she'd had to grow up fast and was twelve by the time she landed on their doorstep, but maybe it was because she was truly different. Not special, like all teenagers dreamed of, just different. She didn't need the attention, or thirst for revenge against everyone who told her to shut up and keep her freaky eyes down. She just wanted to be free to be herself. Free to be like Chance and Shepherd, even if they were both shifters. Or even if they weren't.

Wanting to believe and actually believing were two different things, however.

Maybe she should start with the flashes. A quick peek through her fingers said they were still there. If they were a hallucination, she'd see them whether or not her eyes were closed, meaning they were real.

Mr. Maxen had told her to quit trying so hard not to see what was in front of her.

She let her hands drop and opened her eyes. The flashes seemed calmer, but their random pattern made her twitch, wanting to turn and look away, or to the side. Resolutely, she focused on the nearest object in front of her, the ornate but empty picture frame that had startled her the first time she'd walked through the workroom.

Cautiously, she reached out and touched it. A hazy image began to form and solidified into a watercolor painting. The subject was still a fantasy winter scene of hunting wolves on the trail of a human figure in red and blue, but this time, the wolves were more plentiful and closer to their prey. Three winter-cloaked, crossbow-carrying hunters on galloping horses approached from the left. On the right, a huge, rough statue of a man cast a long shadow, with some sort of big, pale cat creature slinking around the side. A brass plate along the bottom of the picture frame proclaimed the picture's title to be "Choices." She let go of the picture frame, and the image faded, along with the title.

To the left, a black-lacquered box seemed to glow, once she focused her attention on it. It didn't invite her touch like the picture frame had. It felt like it was waiting for someone else, not her.

Several thumps overhead reminded her that she was supposed to be finding the lights out back, not sightseeing in Mr. Maxen's workshop. She shifted her focused gaze up to the back wall and located the switches she'd seen before. She made it several steps down the aisle of low shelves before the flashes started to bother her again. She focused on a candlestick with a candle made of fire that cast a warm glow. She kept her eyes on it for several more steps, then deliberately focused on the next item, a flat, stiletto knife that was about to fall off the shelf. When she pushed it back to safety, the knife seemed to fade a bit. When she grasped its hilt, the whole knife slowly faded from view, leaving only hints of the edges. The ultimate concealed weapon.

By the time she made it to the back wall and the loading dock, the flashes had become less distracting. They were still there, but no longer made her flinch. They seemed more localized, too, as if she could almost figure out which objects were flashing. Maybe they were the magical equivalent of those motion-activated Halloween displays in stores that startled passing shoppers with a cheap sound effect.

When she finally reached the bank of unlabeled switches, she tried them one by one and found three that didn't change any of the lights in the workroom. Unfortunately, whoever created the workroom had removed all of the house's back windows, so she couldn't tell if she was turning on the outside lights or not.

Chance had already turned off the alarm system to let Shepherd in, so it probably wouldn't hurt to raise the loading dock door long enough to check. She opened the slider bar locks on either side, then lifted.

No other lights illuminated the backyard beyond the threshold. She went back to the switches and flipped all three candidate switches, then stepped outside onto the loading dock. The back of the house and the driveway were now gratifyingly well lit. She looked up to the open windows above, but didn't see either Chance or Shepherd.

As she turned to go back in, she saw a glint of something on the ground, a few feet beyond the edge of the concrete. Someone had dropped a rectangular, pocket-sized mirror. She picked it up to take it inside. The back was old, oxidized brass with faint hints of old designs, long since worn away. The surface of the mirror was tinted gold, but her reflected face looked normal enough. She put it in the back pocket of her jeans, since T-shirt designers stupidly chose not to give women chest pockets.

She jerked with sudden pain as something stung the back of her arm. "Yeow!" She lifted her arm to look, and saw little yellow feathers sticking out of her. Before she could move, something stung her thigh, and now it, too, sprouted yellow features. Tranquilizer darts.

Witzer's hunters had found her.

She turned to run back inside, but slipped on the loose gravel and tripped on the edge of the concrete. She landed bruisingly hard on her hands and knees, but scrambled forward. Her arm and thigh already felt cold and numb.

"Grab her!" The hissed words came from the left.

She heard running footsteps. She opened her mouth to scream, only to have a large, rough hand clamp over her face and shove her onto her back. Something crunched under her and stabbed her butt. Her head thumped on the concrete, and she saw stars. She raised her knees and kicked out as hard as she could, connecting with ribs.

"Fuck!" growled a man's voice. She bit the hand that

covered her mouth, causing him to swear again. He made a fist and punched her cheek and nose. Pain exploded in her face and her vision dimmed. The dark-bearded man above her bared his teeth like a predator.

"Get her to the van and come back for me," another man's voice ordered. "I'll take out anyone who comes looking for her."

The feral man smiled cruelly and drew his fist back to hit her again. She whimpered and tried to turn her head aside, but his knee was on her braid.

"Stop that," ordered the other man. "We need her alive. He'll kill us if she's hurt."

The bearded man shot a thin-lipped, frustrated glare at his unseen accomplice, then whipped out a large handkerchief from his pocket and tied it tightly around her head, forcing it into her mouth to gag her.

He threw her over his shoulder and strode off toward the alley. The pressure on her diaphragm made it hard to breathe, and her sore nose bumped his back. The pain in her head made it hard to think. She felt blood dripping from her nose. She couldn't call for Shepherd or Chance, or they'd get shot.

The blood from her nose threatened to block her breathing. She snorted as forcefully as she could, spitefully glad she sprayed blood and snot all down the back of his leather vest.

"Stay still, bitch, or I'll give you another love tap," growled her captor.

"Can't... breathe...." she managed between jarring steps that forced his shoulder into her stomach. She may as well have been talking to the white fence they were walking next to.

A crazy thought burbled up to her increasingly foggy

consciousness. If Shepherd and Chance were shifters, and if the fantasy novels got at least that part right, they'd be able to track her if she left a scent trail. She didn't have any breadcrumbs, but she had blood.

Her kidnapper slowed, and she heard the sound of a panel-van door sliding open. Using her good arm, she reached up and pinched her nose. It hurt like fire, but got her fingers good and bloody.

"Hurry up," ordered a muffled male voice from inside the van. "The timetable is moved up, and they're all coming tonight. We're only a couple of hours ahead of the main force. They already set up the temporary helipad."

As the bearded man shifted his weight, she stretched out her arm to grab the top of one of the white fence's pickets, leaving a dark smear on it before she was wrenched forward, splinters needling into her palm. Her head hit the top of the van as he threw her onto the forward bench seat.

"Oops," he said sarcastically.

*Asshole.* If she could ever afford to pay back her swear fund, she wouldn't have to work for a year.

"Oh my God, Richie, is she dead?" asked a muffled male voice. She slitted her eyes open to see a man wearing a Hawaiian shirt and a full winter facemask. He looked like a convenience store robber on vacation.

"Nah, just dopey from the darts and bleeding a little. Bitches always need obedience lessons." Before she knew what was happening, Richie zip-tied her hands in front of her, then her ankles. "Let's get Adam before he shoots himself and get out of here."

The face-masked man scrambled up to the front. Richie's gaze strayed to her crotch, then upward. He licked his lips as he lingered on her breasts. He shot a furtive glance toward the masked driver, who's attention was elsewhere, and forced her head to the side and leaned down to lick her exposed neck.

She shuddered in revulsion. He reared back with a disgusted snarl. "Fucking hell." He wiped off his tongue with the sleeve of his black T-shirt. "You taste like a goddamn cat." She sent silent, grateful thanks to snuggly little Pandora.

The van started moving. Richie shoved her legs out of the way and sat on the edge of the seat, facing the open van door.

The van seat smelled new, like maybe it was a rental. She surreptitiously turned on her side to face the back cushion and slid her bloody hand into the fold of the seat, hoping she was leaving enough forensic evidence for the police... and maybe the sharper senses of shifters. She'd even take vampires. She really wanted Chance's version of the world to be true.

Her fingers brushed what felt like a wadded paper napkin. While Richie's back was still turned, she gritted her teeth around her gag and deliberately bumped her nose on the seat again, to keep the blood flowing. Her eyes watered involuntarily with the agony of keeping quiet. She eased out the tissue and got it good and wet with her blood, then shoved it back between the cushions.

A cold wave of dizziness washed over her. The overhead light dimmed with her vision.

"Where is he?" asked the driver. "If he's pretending this is a game of Ageless Assassin, I'll kill him."

"Pull into the driveway," said Richie, sounding exasperated. "I'll go find him." He started to leave, then turned back to look at her. He plucked the yellow-feathered dart out of her thigh and the back of her arm and dropped them on the floor. "Check her pockets." He snorted. "Don't want her butt-dialing anyone." Richie launched himself out of the open van door.

Sleepiness eroded her consciousness for long moments.

The van rocked as two men scrambled in and slid the door closed, but she felt too sluggish to turn and look.

"Go, but slow," said Richie. "Don't turn on the lights until we get to the street. And take off those fucking ski-masks. Both of you."

She was glad elderly Mr. Maxen was out of town, out of harm's way.

Maybe once Witzer had her, he'd call off the invasion. Otherwise, the quaint, sleepy little town of Kotoyeesinay wouldn't know what hit it.

She hoped with all her heart that Witzer's goons couldn't find Chance and Shepherd. The last thing she saw was a too-bright reflection on the chrome trim of the overhead light as everything faded to black.

## 7

Chance and Shepherd turned down the narrow alley that led to the now well-lit back entrance of Turn of the Cards. Chance carried the front end of the fifteen-foot steel I-beam, leading the way. Shepherd, with mixed heritage of ogre and bogeyman, could have easily carried it by himself, but he couldn't see well enough at night to avoid taking out fences, shrubs, or spruce trees.

Finally, they reached the driveway. "Let's set it here," said Chance.

Even with borrowing strength from his beast, he was feeling the strain of having carried the heavy beam for four blocks, which was the closest Shepherd could find to park his long truck. They set the beam carefully on the edge of the driveway, next to the rocky strip of the garden. Chance took off his work gloves and shook his hands and shoulders, noting that Moira had left the loading dock door up for them.

"You're stronger than you look," commented Shepherd. "What's your animal, if you don't mind my asking?"

Chance usually dodged the question, but Shepherd was

the closest thing he had to a friend in town. "I don't know, exactly. I'm not a Florida red wolf or a Canadian white cougar, like my parents."

Shepherd nodded. "Oh, a mix, like me. You smell like cat or something."

"Or something," agreed Chance. He pointed to the roll-off bin Shepherd had dropped off. "Let's move this into position while we're here."

Chance watched as Shepherd lifted the bin like it weighed fifty pounds instead of five hundred and placed it a few feet out from the side of the house. Something glinted on the loading dock, and he stepped up to investigate. It was a piece of broken mirror.

As he picked it up, a wave of Moira's magic tickled his senses for a moment, then settled around him like a cloak. He looked around and up, but didn't see her. He liked the feel of her magic on him, and remembered his father, long ago, saying something similar about the feel of his mother's magic. Chance hoped they could find someone to teach Moira to use her talents. He planned to buy her a mirror as a mating gift, because he'd noticed she had an affinity for them.

An errant breeze brought the sour whiff of wolf and unknown human. It had to have been recent, because scents died quickly in the windy, dry summer. Known wolves made Chance's beast wary; unknown wolves made it downright surly. Chance stepped closer to and past the gaping doorway, to see if he could smell it again.

He did, and something far worse. The wolf was ill, and tangled with the wolf's stench was Moira's scent, and a splash of blood. He crouched to wipe it up with his finger, then sniffed it. Human. He touched it to his tongue, memorizing the taste and scent so he could track it. His beast snarled inside, sure that it was Moira's. Whoever had drawn her blood was a dead wolf walking.

"Why are you growling?" asked Shepherd.

"I think Moira's in trouble." He fought his rising beast and clung to his humanity. He needed his ability to talk to get their mate back. "She told me a guy named Witzer was after her, and he sounded like a collector. I thought the town's reputation would keep him away."

Shepherd's normally genial expression turned darkly thunderous. "You go." He pulled out his phone. "I'll call the sheriff and the council."

Chance cast about for Moira's scent and found it, then followed his nose to the alley. Two more drops of blood, then a larger, finer spatter. The scents ended in a scent cloud of engine exhaust, and where a bloody handprint—undoubtedly Moira's from the size and scent—marred a picket of a waist-high white fence. He ran back to Shepherd.

"She's in a vehicle with two human males and an unknown male wolf-shifter who smells of rot. Scent is fresh. We just missed her by ten or fifteen minutes." He pointed toward the alley. "They went northwest, or we'd have seen them."

Shepherd repeated the information into his phone as Chance went back into the well-warded workroom, in case he missed a clue. He ignored the tantalizing magic from dozens of talismans and devices, and focused on using his beast's unrivaled sense of smell. She'd touched several items, but her scent was strongest on the hilt of a flat crystal stiletto that turned transparent when he touched it.

Chance wanted to shift and track, but long experience with unusual occurrences told him he needed to be prepared for more than just a headlong pursuit. He ran quickly up the stairs for his vest and tools, nearly tripping over Moira's backpack. Its presence allayed the tiny worry in the back of his mind that she'd left on her own, but it confirmed his greater fear that she hadn't left willingly. The backpack was her lifeline.

He scooped it into his arms as he clattered down the stairs and out the back again.

Shepherd told him the sheriff was out of town, but Deputy Shiloh was mobilizing the Kotoyeesinay Search and Rescue team of witches and winged shifters to help in the hunt.

"Can you feel each other through your mate bond?" asked Shepherd.

"We're not mated." He ground his teeth in frustration. "She doesn't believe in her own magic, or know what I am, or what you are, or any of this." He paced back and forth, fighting his urge to shift. "I was trying to show her a bit at a time."

Shepherd's phone rang and he answered it. Chance moved closer so he could hear everything.

*"A Jeep passed the town limit, headed north on Trapper Road, then turned on the west ridge trail. It's a maze up in there, near the hot springs."*

Chance shoved his shoulder through one of the straps of Moira's backpack, then picked up his bag of tools. "I know some of the terrain. I'm going in. Tell them not to zap me."

"I'm no good for tracking," said Shepherd. "I'll stay in town."

Chance dug into his jeans pocket and pulled out a slip of paper, which he thrust into Shepherd's ham-sized hand. "Before you go, call Iolo Maxen and ask him how to set the alarms." He saluted Shepherd, then took off at a run toward his truck.

Chance pushed his truck hard on the dry ruts of the dirt road that led to the ridge area, but it still felt slow. He hoped the kidnappers' Jeep had similar limitations. He'd checked in with Shepherd right before he left the range of the town's cell towers. Some incident with tourists in the town was tying up some of the search team, but they'd be there as soon as they could.

In between berating himself for leaving his mate unprotected and for taking her security for granted, he considered his options. Moira's kidnappers undoubtedly had weapons, teams, and directions to their destination, which was more than he had. On the other hand, the wolf that took her was sick with something. Chance had his beast, and the element of surprise. His dark truck would be hard to see, especially since he'd been borrowing his beast's night vision and driving with his lights off.

At every fork and turnoff from the windy road, he had to stop and scent, and hope to hell no one else was around to muck up the trail. At the end of the third switchback, where a steep trail went upward, his nose told him the Jeep had lingered and gone no further. One of the men and the dead wolf walking had taken his mate up the trail. Somehow, he'd missed the Jeep going back down, but it could have taken an off-road trail. He couldn't worry about that now. He had to find Moira. He spent precious minutes turning his truck around and hiding it under a scraggly pine that clung to the steep mountainside. He dragged a dark green canvas tarp out of the back tool locker and draped it over the hood and front grill, to reduce the chance of a reflection giving away the truck's presence.

He left Moira's backpack in the truck, but took his own,

and started up the steep trail. He wanted to roar his challenge to the people who took his woman, who dared to hurt her. Instead, he sent a fervent wish to the silent stars to let her know to hang on, because nothing would stop him from coming for her.

## 8

Lawrence Witzer maintained surface calm as overly muscular, sharp-faced Clay Pruhon, dressed in a silver jumpsuit, climbed into the back seat of Lawrence's custom-built, armored limousine. His driver had parked them in the dirt lot of a salvage yard full of machinery parts, which was as close as they could get to camouflaging its distinctive wide, military shape. He'd paid an exorbitant sum to have it flown in with Pruhon's men, but he was not going to manage an invasion from a surplus infantry mobility vehicle.

Pruhon's alpha power was almost palpable, even to normal people. Lawrence trusted Pruhon's human greed would keep the wolf part of him in check. But just in case, he had positioned quick-acting wolf-shifter tranquilizer guns in multiple locations. The eleven wolves were greedy, hot-headed, and careless, but perfect as secret weapons, hidden among Pruhon's security company of human mercenaries.

"The main operation is going like we planned." Pruhon tapped the microphone in his ear, indicating he'd been in touch with his teams. "But we haven't located Graham yet. The store where my scout tracked her to is dark and closed up tight."

Pruhon's chiding tone rankled, but Lawrence ignored it. He was a much better businessman than Pruhon, and his instincts had urged him to move up the operation by a day. They could catch Graham later, at their leisure. The wolves by themselves had failed to catch her for three years, but after tonight, he'd have a dozen or more psychics under his control.

He'd hardly believed his eyes when he'd watched the video of Graham walking down the street. Divine intervention had Pruhon's scout stopping in the sleepy, foothills tourist-trap for gas, and following Graham's scent into Wyoming and the resort town of Kotoyeesinay.

At first, Lawrence had sneered at the ridiculous names for the businesses that preyed on the gullible, but he'd been struck by a thought. What if Kotoyeesinay held the motherlode of psychics, hidden in plain sight? A quick call to one of his contract sorcerers confirmed that Kotoyeesinay was all Lawrence thought it was and more. It was ripe for the plucking, and Lawrence was just the bold man to do it. They might have psychics, but he had wealth and wolves.

He'd quickly schemed with Pruhon to mobilize his pack and every available human operative to lure the psychics into their snares and spirit them away under the cover of darkness. The high valley on the other side of the mountain was the perfect landing spot for helicopters. He'd keep the best psychics for himself, and quietly auction off the rest.

Lawrence drummed his fingers on the phone that rested on his thigh. "Graham is a lower priority than tonight's mission." He still planned to catch and keep her, however, in case she was still the key to his success. Destiny was sometimes a willful bitch.

Pruhon cleared his throat. "We may have another problem."

"Tell me."

"Your sons went off the radar in Miami two days ago, and we can't find them."

Lawrence drilled Pruhon with his gaze. "And you're just telling me now?"

Pruhon visibly bristled. "I didn't know until a few hours ago. They've been pissy for days, but they really got mad when I removed Richie Traidor, like you ordered. They ditched their security detail. They obviously figured out we'd bugged them, after the last time they pulled that stunt, so they took a taxi to a thrift store and left their clothes in the changing room, then vanished. They aren't losing money in Atlantic City or losing their virginity again in the club in the Dallas, and they aren't having a party at any of your properties."

Adam and Zed had been thorns in his side from the moment they were born, and were constantly plotting harebrained schemes to get control of his companies, instead of waiting their turn like he'd had to do with his father. If they messed up his deal of a lifetime, the one he desperately needed Moira for, he'd feed them to Pruhon's wolves.

"Dammit, I don't have time for their bullshit." Lawrence crossed his arms. "Put Traidor back on their detail. Maybe he can track them down."

"I'll call him in." Pruhon pulled out his phone and rapidly typed a text message.

Lawrence uncrossed his legs. "Back to your report. How many have we got so far?"

"Six. No muss, no fuss, sleeping in the vans." Pruhon's eyes narrowed in thought, and he frowned.

"What?" asked Lawrence.

"Little things. My wolves keep complaining about smelling pine air freshener. The streets are too deserted for a tourist town, except near the casino." He folded his hands together. "I know you paid a lot for the scent and psychic shields, and the 'I'm your best friend' charms for each of us, but this seems too easy."

It was Lawrence's turn to frown. "I see your point." He drummed his fingers. "Let's bring in the rest of the teams now."

"All of them at once in a town this size? That won't be very quiet." Pruhon smiled, clearly pleased by the prospect.

"I don't care. I want to get everyone we can now, and get out. We can sort them out later." Lawrence grinned and pointed to the futuristic helmet in Pruhon's hand. "After all, who's going to believe anyone in a town full of psychics who claim they were abducted by aliens?"

## 9

Moira woke to pain so intense, it blinded her. The hard, sharp surface under her seeped cold into her bones. It took a long minute to determine she wasn't actually blind; she was in a cave with no light. Last she remembered, she'd been in the back cargo area of a Jeep, going up an off-road mountain trail.

The cave smelled dank and musty, like the air didn't circulate well where she was. Thankfully, it didn't smell of critters that made dens in caves. It was warmer than she'd have thought, until she remembered the Wyoming mountains were riddled with hot springs.

She started to sit up, but the agony of her head and neck convinced her to wait a bit. She didn't know whether to blame the tranquilizers, the punch to the face, or the multiple times that Richie had "accidentally" thumped her head against car doors when transferring her in and out of the van and the big-wheeled Jeep.

She curled onto her side and massaged her drum-tight neck as she listened, but heard nothing but her own breathing. She was alone, at least in her part of the cave. *Why* she was alone was something to ponder.

Her arm and thigh were sore from the darts. Even her butt cheek hurt. She slid her arm over her hip and felt with her fingertips. The rectangular shape in her back pocket puzzled her, until she remembered the little brass mirror she'd found in the store's backyard. That must have been the crunch she heard when she'd fought with Richie on the loading dock. Gingerly, she pushed a finger into her pocket and confirmed her fear that the mirror had broken. She likely had shards of it in her ass. Just wonderful.

During the drive, she'd drifted in and out of consciousness as the men had shoved her into the Jeep like a sack of laundry. One of the men stayed with the van in town, and Richie and the third man drove the Jeep up the mountain.

She remembered disjointed bits of conversation that suggested the ski-mask-wearing men were brothers, and they planned to trade her to Witzer for seats on the board of directors. She'd researched Witzer and knew he had dozens of companies and unethical deals, and seemed to prefer the shadows to the spotlight.

One of the brothers had ordered Richie to cut the zip ties off her wrists and ankles, which would have been hard to explain if they got pulled over. They'd repeatedly mentioned "Dad," making her suspect they were Witzer's twin sons, Adam and Zed. She vaguely remembered seeing pictures of them, drunk and falling out of a limousine, on the front page of some checkout-stand scandal rag. She fervently hoped they were as incompetent as they looked.

Darkness didn't scare her, and neither did the twins, but Richie did. He was inhumanly strong—he'd lifted and carried her five-foot-eight frame like she weighed no more than a sweater—and he thrived on violence and pain. Besides, he smelled really bad, like a dog that had rolled in something three-days dead.

She hoped to every deity in existence that Chance and Shepherd had called the sheriff and were coming after her. She missed her backpack, especially her useful tools and her cellphone, but maybe it would convince Chance that she hadn't left by choice.

She guessed she'd only been sleeping for a couple of hours. Her sharp pains were too fresh, and her muscles weren't sore yet from overexertion. She rolled onto her back and reached out with her arms. More uneven, cold rock underneath her. To her left, her fingertips brushed a vertical surface of rock. Ignoring the eye-watering pain of her head, she felt around with both hands and feet. They'd apparently stashed her for safekeeping next to the wall in a small cul-de-sac of the cave. She didn't feel very safe.

The stabbing sensation in her butt motivated her to gently fish out the broken pieces of mirror in her back pocket and put them aside so she wouldn't roll on them again. Finally, she slid the frame itself out. From what her fingers told her, only one curved corner remained. Too bad it didn't flash like the mirrors in the shop, or she could use it to see how to get the hell out of the cave.

She nearly dropped the frame when the mirror started to glow, low at first, then bright enough to dazzle her dark-adapted eyes. She put it facedown on her chest to shade it. When she looked in the corner of the cave, the smaller shards were softly glowing like a little string of Christmas lights.

Great. She was now completely and totally crazy. Off the deep end. Certifiable.

But if crazy meant she had magic, and a broken mirror

could give off enough light to get her out of the cave without falling down some inconvenient shaft, she'd take it. Reality was overrated.

In the real world, she'd be powerless to get away from Richie, and stuck being a pawn in the Witzer family power struggle. In the magical world, she had the means to escape and find her way back to a man she was falling in love with, despite having met him only two days ago. She just hoped they hadn't shot him.

Which reminded her of overhearing the twins laughing about how their father would soon be busy with Richie's security team, rounding up all the psychic wackos in Kotoyeesinay. Witzer would hurt anyone who got in the way of his quest to get to her. She had to warn them.

She took a deep breath, tucked her braid down the back of her T-shirt, then started crawling, using her mirror light to show her the way. The passage opened up into a wider, taller portion, meaning she could stand and walk for a while. Her head was feeling marginally better, but her nose was stuffy and ached. Even if her nose wasn't broken, she'd bet she had one hell of a black eye starting. How sexy.

The larger cave was chilly, and seemed to have ventilation from somewhere. Every few yards, she stopped to listen for any other sounds, but heard nothing. She couldn't guess why they hadn't tied her up again or taken her shoes, or at least left a guard, unless they trusted the total darkness to keep her prisoner. As it would have, without her miraculous... no, *magic* mirror.

When she crouched to examine one of two possible passageways, wondering which one would take her to freedom, her mirror pulsed red. The green pulse when she pointed the mirror toward the other passageway was good enough for her. Just as she was resting and listening, wishing for some kneepads, she thought she saw a glimmer of light at the end of the passage, which spurred her to move faster. The last place she wanted to be caught was in a four-foot-high passage with no place to hide or run.

Once again, the cave opened wide. The light turned out to be a heavy-duty, club-style flashlight. She bet someone had left it to point to the correct passage. She switched it off and shoved it in her back waistband. If nothing else, it would make a good weapon. The front button of her pants gave way and made a metallic pinging sound as it bounced out of view. She sighed, knowing her jeans were history. It was so hard to find a pair that fit. A whiff of herself said she'd probably have to burn her T-shirt.

This part of the cave system was cluttered with gray rocks, and she felt a breeze tickle the hair on the back of her neck. When she finally saw the cave's entrance, she shut off her mirror light by the simple expedient of shoving the frame in her front pocket. Or she would have, if it hadn't already been occupied by Chance's bandanna. It gave her the idea to rig a pocket sling around her neck to hold the mirror high on her chest, so she'd have two hands for climbing. She used the hair tie from the end of her braid to secure it. The mirror blazed brightly when faced outward, and dowsed when faced toward her chest.

The ground beyond the cave entrance sloped down sharply. As much as she needed to get out of the cave and warn Chance and the town, she'd likely break her neck if she went sliding down a steep mountainside in the dark. The high surrounding peaks blocked any help from the moonlight. She flipped the mirror forward long enough to pick a path, then eased over to the left and grabbed onto a branch of a crooked scrub pine. Dirt and pine needles slid out from under her, making her scramble for footing and send a cascade of pebbles downward.

The windy mountain wasn't as quiet as the cave, but if her captors were anywhere near and heard her creating miniature landslides, they'd catch her for sure. The only thing she could think of was to make her way down from one tree or shrub to the next, using her mirror light just long enough to pick her targets.

She just reached a bulbous granite outcrop when she heard a voice echoing.

"Here's the second marker." That was Richie.

"Where are the twidiots?" She didn't recognize the voice.

Richie laughed. "Twidiots. That's good. Adam lost his keys, and Zed went back to town to pick him up. I called Pruhon as soon as Zed left, but you don't have much time to get her out of here before they come back."

A passing beam of light briefly outlined the ridge of rocks below her.

It was too late to think about going up the mountain, but the big rock might hide her in the dark. She pushed her way around it and past a low shrub, feeling with her foot rather than her vulnerable hands. Her shoe and pant leg might offer protection if she disturbed a sleeping snake. Shuddering at the thought, she pushed aside the tough branches of a shrub to squeeze in beside it, making herself as small as possible. The flashlight pushed on her kidney, and the zipper of her jeans dug into her skin. Fortunately, any noise she'd made was covered by the scrape of feet and grunts of effort from the two men.

If they went by her and into the cave, she could sneak down the mountain by following their path. She pulled her T-shirt over her knees, then ducked her head so her face and eyes wouldn't be visible. She hoped her gray T-shirt made her huddled form look like a piece of the rock. She felt a stir of wind that left a coating of... something on her. Maybe it was her imagination, but she hoped it was her magic, hiding her.

She tracked them by sound and the occasional quick glance to check their progress. The stench of filthy, wet dog stung her sore nose, even through the congestion.

The man with the flashlight hesitated in front of the cave entrance that Richie pointed to. "You said she's a witch. She's not going to shrivel my nuts or anything, is she?"

"Hell, Chaffet, how could you tell the difference?" Richie laughed when the other man growled. "She's no threat. Adam double-tranqued her with that gun he lifted from Witzer's limo. She's an ordinary human. She'll be out for hours. Muzzle her when you get her in the van, though. She can make your ears bleed with her scream."

Chaffet ducked and went in. Richie started to follow, then stopped and turned, his face tilted up like he was smelling something. He shook his head, then ducked inside.

She wished she knew how her magic worked, so she could trap them in the cave. She tried willing rocks above the entrance to slide, but they stayed stubbornly still. She didn't have any more time to waste, so she slowly extricated herself from the branches.

She listened intently as she crab-walked quietly toward the gap in the rocky ledge, then oozed down, feeling with her feet. She flipped her mirror light briefly for a snapshot view of the trail, then flipped it over again and eased down the steep slope on her butt as far as she dared in the dark, then repeated the sequence. She hoped anyone below would assume the light was from Chaffet's flashlight.

Come to think of it, she had her own flashlight, stuffed in her pants, but she preferred her mirror. Her magic. It sounded weird but felt true. God, she hoped she'd get to tell Chance he was right.

By the time she reached a flatter section of the slope, she shook with a combination of terror and fatigue. Her athletic shoes didn't have the best traction, and she nearly slipped into a bed of sharp rocks and the painful-looking branches of a dead tree. Each sound made her jump, sure that another of Richie's pals was waiting to grab her. She couldn't leave their back trail, or she'd never find the road. It had been hard enough to follow their footprints over the sections of solid rock, but her mirror light helped by pulsing green when she pointed it the right direction.

Where she crouched, the ground was sandier, probably deposits from rain runoff. She occasionally heard water trickling somewhere as she'd made her descent. If flash floods had a season, she hoped it wasn't early June.

An angry shout echoed off the rocks and peaks. No telling where it came from, but odds were good for above, near the cave. Her mirror light showed her the path to the wide slot between two tall rock outcroppings, but the second she took a step in that direction, the mirror pulsed red.

It pulsed green when she turned it to the right. She stifled the little voice that said she was imagining things. She didn't care, as long as it kept her alive. A thicket of scrub oak loomed before her.

A scrape against branches was all the warning she had before a hand clamped over her mouth and she was pulled into a hard man's body.

She bit, elbowed, and stomped, squirming to get away.

"Ow! It's me!" whispered Chance in her ear, removing his hand from her mouth.

Her knees gave way with a flood of relief.

"I've got you." His arms surrounded her for one long, blissful moment. "Sorry I scared you."

As much as she wanted to sink into his solid warmth, they needed to leave. Crying into his shirt again could come later.

"Two men above." She stood up straight and squared her shoulders. "They think I'm a witch. They want to kidnap me from the kidnappers."

"Two men below, too. Are you okay?" He rubbed her arms up and down.

"Nothing a shower, an ice pack, and a couple of aspirin can't fix. Any idea how to get out of here?"

"Yep." He slid his hand into hers and tugged. She followed, comforted by the fact he seemed to have a plan. She noticed he wore a backpack, and felt a pang for hers.

The slope started to rise, and she couldn't see a thing. She started to turn her mirror around, then hesitated. Chance could apparently see just fine, and she might ruin his night vision.

A wailing wolf call echoed off the rocks.

Chance turned and scooped her up into his arms and tight against his chest before she knew what was happening. "Hang on tight." She grabbed for his neck as he began running swiftly up the slope.

In pitch black.

Like she weighed next to nothing.

Little pieces of the puzzle clicked into place. The man she wanted more than luxury chocolate was a shifter. A magical mix of man and animal. And he wasn't the only one.

"I think the men up top might be, er, wolves. Shifters."

He stumbled, but recovered and kept going. "You're okay with that?"

"Hell, no. They stink. They probably want to eat me or hump me. And not the fun way, either." Just the thought of Richie pawing her nauseated her.

His hold tightened, and she felt a growl emanate from his chest. "You're mine."

Possessiveness usually turned her off, but not from him. "Yes. And you're mine." For as long as she could stay without endangering him.

They crested the slope and plunged down into a rockier section. She heard the gurgle of water somewhere below. He pushed off with powerful legs, and suddenly, they were flying through the air, until he landed with a stomach-flipping dip and took two steps, then jumped again. She wanted to see, but was glad she couldn't, or she'd have given away their position with little shrieks. She'd have had to give back her fearless princess card.

Once they hit the bottom of the ravine, he plunged into the shallows of a splashing stream and ran until he came to more rocks, then jumped again. He barely seemed winded when he finally set her down. "I think we lost them. I parked my truck on the trail access road just on the other side of this rise."

"Did you call the sheriff?" She stomped quietly to get some circulation back into her legs.

"Yes. Help is coming, but not right away, and I couldn't wait." He lightly brushed her swollen cheekbone with his thumb. "I'll kill whoever did this to you."

She couldn't see his expression, but the undercurrent of wildness in his tone made her want to kiss him. Her newly perky hormones apparently didn't care that they were still in mortal danger.

"His name's Richie, but he's not worth killing. Maiming, maybe." She sighed. "Witzer will just send more."

"We'll deal with him next." He kissed her, then came back for seconds. He slid his hands down to her waist and around, then stopped. He patted her lower back. "What's this?"

"Flashlight. Richie stashed me deep in a cave, then left it out front as a marker."

"How did you get out?" He took her hand in his and started walking. "Rock to your right at two-o'clock."

She moved closer to him. "Luck." She made herself say the rest. "And magic."

He was silent for a few strides. "And you're okay with that, too?"

She knew his real question was whether or not she'd accept him. "More than okay. It saved me." She squeezed his hand. "You saved me."

"Working on... Down!"

He pulled her on top of him so fast her head spun. It didn't help that he rolled them several times sideways, landing next to a small clump of an evergreen shrub, his rock-hard body atop hers. The tension in his body kept her quiet as a church mouse. After several long, silent moments, she heard a low whirring sound, but couldn't see anything but Chance's broad chest. A flash of memory reminded her how lickable his chest was, and how much he liked that. *Later,* she admonished herself.

"Four-propeller drone with a searchlight and a camera," Chance whispered in her ear. "Question is, friend or wolf?"

She guessed he wasn't feeling any more charitable toward wolves than she was. An idea bubbled up. Mr. Maxen seemed to think she had a gift for knowing the truth. "Let me see it. Maybe I can tell."

He rolled slowly aside. She craned her head until a flash caught her attention, and she found the drone.

So far, her magic had worked based on need, on goals, like getting out of the cave and hiding. They needed to escape, meaning they *needed* to know who operated the drone. She imagined an invisible tethering thread, then traced it back to its source. An image came to her, hazy at first, of a joystick, operated by a man, intent on a display screen. He appeared to be in a van. On instinct, she looked at the man through the van's rear view mirror, and saw an overlay of lupine features.

She shook her head to clear the vision, and sternly squelched the little voice that said it was just her vivid imagination running wild again. "Wolf. I think. I'm still finding my way with magic." She congratulated herself for not stumbling over the word this time.

He tightened his arms around her a moment. "It will come."

They watched as the flashing drone followed a zigzag pattern down the hill where they'd come up. It occurred to her she might be prejudiced by her limited bad experience. "Are there good wolves?"

"Your chest is glowing."

"Huh?" She looked down. Her light was face down in its makeshift sling, but glowing around the edges of the frame. "Mirror. It's how I got out of the cave." It faded as she spoke.

Maybe her use of magic had energized it, which meant she'd really worked magic, and a wolf really was operating the drone. That was her theory, and she was sticking to it.

## 10

Chance could barely hang onto his control. His body wanted to mate with the woman under him right then and there. His beast wanted to shred the wolves. His human brain wanted to find out what had opened her mind to the world of magic, and help her explore it. His survival instinct said shut up and get moving while the drone was out of sight.

She'd asked a question. "Some wolves are good," he admitted grudgingly, "but none of the ones up here are. The ones I smelled are all sick." He rose to his knees and helped her stand. "We need to run. Can I carry you? I'm sorry, I should have asked last time."

She smiled. "You're forgiven for saving my life." She kissed his jaw, then raised her arms. "Let's go."

Her trust humbled him. He scooped her into his arms and ran, coming close to half shifting to achieve maximum speed over rocky terrain in the dark.

He stopped at the crest of the final hill that would take them down to the dirt road where his truck was hopefully still hidden. He let her legs drop to the ground and supported her shoulders until she was standing on her own. "My truck's close, but I want to scout around first."

The waning moonlight lit the flatter terrain, which was all he'd need to see by. He could go lightning fast without Moira, but he didn't want to leave her unprotected with greedy, hungry wolves in the area. His dilemma must have shown on his face.

"I'll hide under that tree—at least I think it's a tree—so you can go." She gave him a smartass grin. "I'll rescue you if you get in trouble."

She scooted under the tree and waved him away. "The sooner you go, the sooner you're back." She wrapped her arms around her knees, and he felt her magic flare. He still couldn't tell what it was doing.

He melted into the night, staying in human form because it was less obvious, and because he was afraid to show Moira his other form without giving her some warning first. She was a brave woman, but she was still getting used to the idea of shifters. Who knew what she'd think of him?

He circled twice and found no footprints or scents other than his own. As far as he could tell, his truck was undisturbed, and neither he nor his beast could stand leaving his mate unprotected any longer.

He nearly had a heart attack when he didn't see or smell her at first, but then he felt a little breeze of magic, and suddenly, she was right where he'd left her.

"Did it work? Was I hidden?"

"Yes, even to my nose." He waited until she stood and brushed off the seat of her pants to give her a quick kiss. "You're beautiful by moonlight."

She gave him a wry smile. "You're crazy, but you're cute." She tilted her head toward the hill. "Can we go home now?"

She looked hopeful, then frowned. "Unless those a-holes blew up Mr. Maxen's store."

"The store has protection." He held out his hand. "Let's go."

He opened the truck for her and dropped his backpack behind the seat, then set about removing the camouflage brush and tarps.

She beamed at him when he slid into the driver's seat and started the engine. Her smile went straight to his groin. He was not a wolf, dammit, with uncontrollable urges. He gripped the wheel tighter.

"Thank you for bringing my backpack." She'd already pulled on her hoodie and zipped it. The tiny mirror decorations across the hood, shoulders, and sleeves briefly reflected the truck's overhead courtesy light.

"You're welcome. I should have brought you a jacket for the cold." He slowly pulled his truck into the ruts of the dirt road and started down.

"I'm not that cold. I grew up just south of the Canadian border, so I'm used to this." She patted the sleeve of her hoodie. "I just wanted to feel, I don't know, better armored."

He glanced at her. "It's the mirrors."

"You think?" She held out her arm and looked at them. "Huh." She put her arm down. "I bought this the last day of the Renaissance fair. The lady sold it to me for half price because some of the mirrors had come off. That was my favorite part of the design, so I taught myself to embroider so I could fix it. I kind of got carried away." She sighed. "I wonder if that was my magic, or just luck?"

He slowed to take the first hairpin turn, wishing he had an answer for her. Maybe they could figure it out together when they got back to Kotoyeesinay.

"Wouldn't driving be easier with the lights... never

mind." She was silent for a long moment. "Is it rude of me to ask what kind of shifter you are? All I have to go by is fantasy novels, and they're all over the map as far as customs and biology and stuff. I hope that full-moon silliness isn't real."

"It isn't, but unmated wolves use it as an excuse to get laid." He sped up again, until they were bouncing along at a bone-jarring pace. "I think the light of a full moon made it easier for ordinary people to see careless shifters who didn't check that no one was around when they changed form."

"That makes sense." She crossed her arms. "What did you mean earlier about the wolves being sick? They smell bad, even to my stuffed-up nose, but dogs are always rolling in stinky things."

Chance chuckled. "Wolves are *not* dogs, they'll have you know." He shook his head. "I have a nose for detecting illness. I'd need to get closer to them to be sure, but all the faint scents I've been picking up smell like the wolves are half dead. Shifters don't get human diseases, so I suspect someone, probably their alpha, is stealing their life essence."

"Why would he do that? Doesn't it weaken his pack?"

"Power. I knew of a pack where the alpha stayed on top by blood-bonding with his pack and siphoning off their strength. He told them they were cursed by a Native American shaman to explain why the rest of the pack kept dying of old age in their first century. He was nearly eleven hundred when he was killed." It was his maternal grandmother's favorite story, about how she and her cougar shifter clan had put an end to the alpha wolf's reign of terror. It had also turned the cougars and the wolves in the Yukon into mortal enemies to this day.

"Are shifters born or made?" Her tone had a thread of wariness.

"Both." He knew she needed the truth, unpleasant as it could be. "And yes, it's possible to force the change on compatible humans. Most shifters find the thought appalling, worse than rape or slavery, but there are always a few."

Another turn took his attention, meaning he couldn't see how she was taking his revelations.

"Just like people, I guess. Most are good, but bad people make the headlines." She sounded sad.

He wanted to reassure her, or at least touch her, but he needed both hands to drive. "It can't be done by accident, like with a scratch or a bite, if that's what you're worried about. It takes deliberate intent by both human and beast, and takes a couple of days."

She was silent after that. He wished he knew what she was thinking, but driving fast in the dark took concentration.

Out of the corner of his eye, he saw her pick up the heavy flashlight she'd confiscated and lean down to slide it into her backpack.

Oddly, the little mirrors on her sleeves started to glow red.

"Shit." She grabbed onto the dashboard in front of her. "Pick a new direction, because we're headed toward trouble."

He braked as hard as he dared on the uneven road, then cranked the wheel. The back wheels fishtailed alarmingly as he punched the accelerator.

The mirrors on her hoodie stayed red.

He slammed on the brake, fumbling with her seatbelt. "West. Up the hill. I'll be right behind you."

She grabbed her backpack and gave him a scared look before opening the door and scrambling out. Her magic flared, and her mirrored hoodie went dark, almost as if the mirrors were casting shadows on her, making her harder to see. He put the truck in park and grabbed the keys, then launched himself out the open passenger door, slowing just long enough to shut the door. He caught up to her and helped her up the incline, then scooped her into his arms again.

"Stop right there, hero." The loud command dripped with sarcasm and menace.

Three men flicked on flashlights and emerged from the darkness, carrying rifles. The biggest man wore a beard and a sneer. The blond next to him looked antsy, and the older, gray-haired man on the end looked bored. They had the preternatural silence of predator shifters, but they also had no scent. Chance felt a frisson of Moira's magic, and necklaces on each of the men briefly glowed. Suddenly, he got a noseful of wolf shifter scent. Definitely blood-bound wolves, from the sinus-clearing bad odor of death. Her magic must have overpowered whatever concealment talismans they were using.

A night owl's hunting cry pierced the night. All three men glanced at it, then back to Chance. He hunched his shoulders diffidently and willed them to dismiss him as an ordinary human. Thanks to the magic in his blood, they couldn't scent him unless he let them.

The bearded man pointed at Moira. "Give us the woman and get lost."

Chance tightened his arms, but she put a firm hand on his chest. "They want me, not you." She closed her eyes. Her magic flared and settled like a fine net on his skin.

"Listen to her, pal," said the blond man. "We don't care

about you. She's a witch and a shifte--*oof!*" His words cut off when the biggest man elbowed him hard.

The bearded man crossed his arms. "She's a shifty thief. Now hand her over."

Chance reluctantly let her down. She stumbled to one knee, and he bent low to catch her.

"You're hidden, like I was. I hope." she breathed in his ear. "Find me."

She straightened up, and as she did, her backpack faded into a shadowed outline. Without a backward glance, she walked calmly toward the bearded man. Her mirrored hoodie seemed to reflect the flashlights. She walked right up to him and dick-punched him, hard.

He collapsed to his knees, wheezing.

"Hit me again, Richie, and you'll need both hands to piss." She opened her fist and blew a handful of rock dust into his face. "Now I won't even have to touch you."

She turned to the blond man. He raised his rifle. "Keep away from me." He backed into the older man, who snarled and shoved him off.

Chance honored Moira's gift of a distraction by using it. He crouched and leapt high and to the side, onto the eight-foot-tall boulder. He crouched again, then jumped twice more to the higher rocks behind it, giving him a bird's eye view of the action.

"Where the fuck did he go?" growled the blond man. "He can't have gone far."

"Later. You two take her to the van," Richie wheezed. "Pruhon expected her in the holding cell by midnight, and that was an hour ago. I'll take care of the human, then find the Witzer brats." Richie climbed to his feet and handed his rifle to the older man. "Take this, or Adam will want to play with it and probably shoot his foot off."

The blond man waved his gun to indicate the slope that led to the road. "Walk, bitch, or we'll tie you like a turkey and drag you."

They disappeared from view, but Chance saw the beam of a flashlight and heard the shuffling of feet as they stepped onto the packed dirt road.

"Chaffet," said Moira in a loud, overly sweet voice, "Underwear too tight on your nuts? Shove me again, and I'll shrink them to fit."

"How do you know my name?" Suspicion mingled with fear in the man's tone.

She laughed. "The same way I know the van is about a mile down the road, on the hill above it, with one asshole inside, jacking off to Internet porn. I hope none of the rest of you touches that joystick, because, *ewww*." Bless his clever, magical mate for her bravery.

"She's a witch, you dumbfuck." The older wolf sounded disgusted.

"Fuck you, Washenko."

Chance focused on Richie, whose shifter metabolism had undoubtedly already healed whatever pain Moira had caused in his genitals. His body language said he was trying to pick up Chance's trail without shifting. Richie was no alpha, so he didn't have half-shift capabilities, but most shifters, even sick ones, had better senses than the average human. He looked left, right, and behind him, then turned quietly to his left and walked southward, leading with his nose.

Richie could wait. The two twitchy wolves with guns on his mate had first priority.

Chance left the rocks and ran swiftly north, then crossed the road and headed southwest, trusting the net of Moira's magic to help conceal him.

Once he got closer to the van, he discovered more men deployed in a large defensive circle. Judging by the first two he'd found, they couldn't see each other, but were in constant communication via radio and headsets. He couldn't smell them, meaning they probably wore concealment charms like Chaffet and Washenko had. They all had a military air about them, and plenty of firepower.

Time to even the odds.

Moira told herself she wasn't afraid, but she'd never been good at lying to herself. The breath of her escorts exuded a stench of carrion, like they hadn't eaten fresh meat in months, Chaffet especially. Only their fear of her witchy powers and their greater fear of Pruhon, their pack leader, kept them from hurting her.

On the know-thy-enemy principle, she focused her knowing magic on the two men... no, wolves in men's clothing, but she couldn't tell if it helped. She'd already figured out that Chaffet was a sly whiner and not very bright, and that Washenko hid feral savagery under a thin veneer of civility. The magic charms they wore, the ones she'd instinctively disabled, were easier to discern as coming from a disdainful sorcerer for hire who sold the cheaper goods to no-talent humans and numbskull shifters because they wouldn't know the difference.

As much as her instincts urged her to run, she doubted her magic was strong enough to hide her from inhumanly fast, inhumanly strong wolves with guns. Not to mention, she didn't have shifter night vision to find her way in the dark. Her only assets were her wits, luck, and, she hoped, Chance.

"So," she said conversationally, "how does it work in your pack? Does your alpha get first crack at me, or am I someone's reward?" She hoped she sounded like she didn't care that they probably intended to hurt her or worse.

"Mates weaken wolves," said Chaffet loftily. "We're selling you to the highest bidder."

"Oh, stealing me from Witzer, then." She shrugged elaborately. "Your business, of course, but take it from me, he's definitely the type to hold a grudge."

"Nah, he'll blame his scheming sons for losing you, and because you're a witch, too, we'll get a million for you, easy." Chaffet grinned. "Win-win."

"You talk too much," grumbled Washenko.

Moira agreed, and took advantage of it. She discovered they planned to fly her out of the mountains in a helicopter, then use their private company jet to deliver her to the auction winner like she was a mail-order package. When Richie had helped the twins kidnap her, he'd discovered she was a witch with shifter-mate potential, and notified Pruhon of her real value. Richie and Chaffet used their satellite phone to report she was missing from the cave, and Pruhon sent Washenko and the others to hunt her. She didn't want to expose her ignorance by asking what the hell "shifter-mate potential" meant, and how they knew. Which in turn made her wonder if Chance knew, and if so, why he hadn't told her. Unless it was only for stinky wolves, in which case, yuck.

"Shut up for a minute," ordered Washenko. "I haven't heard any radio chatter for the last ten minutes, and Dorsey isn't answering." He powered his shoulder radio off and on.

Chaffet waved dismissively. "Probably fucking with the drone." He tapped a button on his radio. "Hey, Cho Lai, if you're dry-humping a juniper, I'm not pulling the needles out of your dick."

They grew more alert with the ensuing silence.

"Richie seems fond of double-crossing people," Moira observed, hoping to sow doubt.

Chaffet growled his denial and raised his gun, eyes tracking from side to side.

Washenko looked more thoughtful, but raised his gun, too.

A not-so-distant animal roared in the night. Chaffet instantly spun to his right and shot into the dark, only missing Washenko's eyebrow by inches.

Moira dove to the ground, skinning her already sore palms, but Washenko hauled her back up again. "Give me that!" He snatched Chaffet's gun and shoved her at him. "Hold her," he snarled. "She's our insurance."

Washenko slung two of the rifles onto his shoulder and pointed the barrel of the third into the side of her neck. "The van."

Chaffet held his flashlight with one hand and painfully squeezed the back of her neck with the other the other to frog-march her down the road. Washenko kept pace and maintained pressure with the barrel. She stumbled along as best she could, knowing they'd hurt her if she didn't cooperate.

Growls from fighting wolves erupted to the right, then a pained yelp, then silence.

Chaffet chanted a litany of obscenities under his breath. Washenko vibrated with tension as they left the road and started up a rock-strewn slope. A brief flash of light illuminated the top of the hill and the van, right before it exploded into a fireball.

Chaffet stumbled and pulled her backward, away from

Washenko's gun. His flashlight went flying. She threw herself to the side and tripped over a rock. As she fell to her hands and knees, Washenko raised his rifle to aim at a dark shape coming down the slope at them. The unconscious, slashed body of a huge gray wolf slammed into him and Chaffet, knocking them over like bowling pins.

Moira crawled away as fast as she could, but she got tangled in a pair of black pants crumpled on the ground. A hand clamped onto her ankle and hauled her backward. She took in a lungful of air, then turned and screamed, banshee loud and long.

The hand let go. "My ears!" cried Chaffet. He and Washenko both howled in pain as she crawled away again and climbed to her feet, but tripped over a rifle barrel.

She pulled the mirror light out of her T-shirt and turned it around. Before she could take a step, a fist slammed into her stomach. "No more screaming, bitch!"

She folded to her knees, her diaphragm temporarily stunned. She fought to draw in a ragged breath, then she nearly threw up from the unmistakable rotting stench of Richie. It didn't help that he was naked and beginning to sprout dark fur. In seconds, a larger-than-nature gray wolf stood in his place, wetly gleaming teeth bared, growling, and preparing to lunge at her.

She focused on her mirrors, flaring them bright to blind him. As he shook his massive head, she grabbed the thick barrel of the heavy rifle and swung the stock, two-handed, against his skull. He yelped in pain and backed up, shaking his head. She took another swing at him.

She tripped on a boot, and the heavy stock went under his chin and slammed into his throat. He coughed and backed up a few more steps, shaking his head. Before she could line up for a third strike, his body was knocked sideways with a meaty thump by something big, tawny-colored, and fast. They tumbled down the slope, out of the pool of light her mirror cast.

She flared her mirror light and ran with the rifle, across the slope, away from the angry wolves. Every step jarred her sore stomach muscles. She staggered to the base of a rock and leaned against it with one arm, coaxing her legs and lungs not to give up. The sound of a gunshot made her quickly douse her light and use her hiding magic to avoid becoming a target.

She heard human shouts and animal growls, and then a long, heart-rending, pained animal whine that ended in silence. It was easier to take when she remembered Richie transforming into a big slavering wolf that wanted to rip her throat out.

Another gunshot rang out. "Goddamn it, Chaffet, you fucking shot me!" Washenko sounded more aggrieved than injured.

"It wasn't me," whined Chaffet, somewhere below Washenko's voice. "I don't have a gun."

"I do." Chance's voice rang with authority and confidence. "If you want to live, sit down and stay human."

A flashlight flickered on, illuminating Chaffet and Washenko on the side of the hill, about fifteen feet apart. They both looked filthy and battered. Between them, a tail and hind paw were all that were visible of Richie's wolf form. Even as she watched, the tail vanished and the paw morphed into a naked human foot.

"He can't be dead," said Chaffet, clearly shaken. "The blood exchange with Alpha Pruhon makes us immortal."

"It only makes *him* immortal," said Chance. "It's killing the pack. Every time you shift, he takes a piece of you. Richie wouldn't have lasted another year."

"Bullshit," growled Washenko, his voice sounding more wolf than human. His face began to elongate as he ripped his shirt open. His neck sprouted dark fur as muscles rippled underneath the skin. But instead of changing into a wolf, the way Richie had, Washenko clutched at his chest with clawed hands and sank to his knees.

Chaffet howled and dropped to his knees as well, then collapsed in a boneless heap.

Washenko lasted a few moments longer, his expression a mix of anger and pain, before falling forward like a sack of grain.

Chance flickered the flashlight in her direction, waving it uncertainly. "Moira?"

"Here." She released her hiding magic and briefly flared her mirror light.

He crossed to her at a half-run and wrapped her in a brief embrace, then pulled back. "Are you hurt?" It was the first time she'd seen him look scared.

"Only sore. You?" Just because he seemed invincible didn't mean he couldn't be hurt. "And what about them?" She pointed toward where Washenko and Chaffet lay.

"I'm good. I knocked out the guards and blew up their van. All the wolves are dead, or as good as, including those two." He tilted his head toward the bodies. "I felt Pruhon draining them. He must be under attack."

She remembered Chaffet's earlier chatter. "Oh my God, the town! We have to warn them. Witzer and Pruhon brought in a hundred mercenaries to round up psychics to sell on the black market. They'll be no match for a military invasion."

"I haven't been here that long, but from what I've seen, it's more likely that Witzer's mercenaries will be no match for the town." He shook his head. "I think you have the same luck as I do for the downright unusual, except you look at it as an adventure."

She wanted to kiss him, but knew she'd never stop if she did. "Not really. I just like helping people when they need it."

He gave her a tender smile. "I used to think of my luck as a curse, but I wouldn't have met you without it." He kissed her forehead. "Let's go see if we can help."

With her consent, he carried her toward where they'd left his truck. He seemed to like holding her, and she liked being held for a bit. Even princesses could use a breather after marching all over the mountains.

It was a warm, wonderful feeling to know that Chance considered her an asset in a fight. Of all the things she still didn't know about him, such as what kind of animal he turned into, or how old he really was, or if he liked breakfast for dinner, she did know one thing. She'd fallen in love with the man, and it would rip her heart out if she had to leave him.

## 11

L awrence Witzer barely kept from swearing out loud when the cuff of his pants tore on the loose board hanging off a picket fence he was moving past. Some might call it skulking, but traversing dark alleys at two in the morning carrying a wolf tranquilizer gun, regardless of the city, called for stealth. The sound of children laughing and a swimming pool splash motivated him to move faster.

He'd wanted to leave hours ago, but one damned thing after another skewed his plans. He suspected destiny was putting him through trials to see if he was truly worthy, and it pissed him off. He'd paid his dues—not to mention, paid greedy sorcerers and Pruhon's company—and he deserved results.

First, Pruhon's pack had caught his moronic sons on the outskirts of Kotoyeesinay, headed west into the high country. Lawrence hadn't for a second believed their lame story of coincidentally visiting the exclusive casino, but he didn't have time to get the truth out of them. He ordered Pruhon to lock them up for later.

Second, they lost the main containment area, which they'd dressed up as an alien landing site. Pruhon's operatives set it up in the narrow park as planned, and when he and Pruhon had checked on it an hour later, it was gone, along with the psychics they'd collected and twenty spacesuit-wearing, military-trained men.

They'd lost another landing site right after he'd visited it. Two little old ladies had approached him outside the convenience store where he'd stopped to use the restroom. They said their crystal ball told them he was the person to ask about meeting the aliens, which they both had always dreamed of. He'd given them a ride in his limo to the smaller site near the mobile home park. He wasn't supposed to be part of the sweeper operation, but it would be stupid to turn away destiny's gifts.

When he'd walked them to the theatrically glowing fence, they'd become quite animated.

"I hope they're big and blue, and never wear their shirts... Oh, Jane, look at that spaceship! It's even better than that movie, you know, the one with the music."

In the better light of the security perimeter, Lawrence noticed both women wore 1950s-style housedresses and had conservatively coiffed but brilliant blue hair that would put his pathetic son's green-tipped hair to shame.

"I know the one," agreed Jane, "With that guy, and the mashed potatoes." She waved toward the "ship" partially hidden with a manufactured fog. "This one looks a lot smaller."

Bertha turned to Lawrence with a wide-eyed gaze. "Do you think they'd let us have a look inside?"

Lawrence hid a smile. "It couldn't hurt to ask." He pointed to the spacesuit-wearing alien near the disguised truck. Just like taking candy from a baby.

When he went back twenty minutes later, that site was gone, too.

Psychics had been harder to find after that. Pruhon's pack had to use precious time in tracking down home addresses, since most of the shops had closed early. That, Lawrence put down to the psychics using their talents. He couldn't explain why Pruhon's operatives steadily dwindled in numbers, to where by midnight, they had less than thirty experienced, armed mercenaries to control the town.

Pruhon became angrier as the night wore on, especially after some of his pack disappeared along with the mercenaries. He growled about being able to locate them, but not access them, whatever that meant. In the relatively small confines of the limo, Pruhon smelled like roadkill, and became increasingly antsy. Around two o-clock, Witzer finally ordered Pruhon out to go find his wolves, because otherwise, there would be no putting up with him. Lawrence wished he hadn't watched the man as he'd shifted. "Never" would be too soon to see the man's ugly junk again. Or his furry ass, for that matter.

Lawrence's finely-honed self-preservation instincts said he needed to leave, but he had one more card to play. His horribly expensive sorcerer had come through with a home address for where Moira Graham was staying. All he needed to do was slip into the house, tranq her, and carry her out to his limo waiting out front.

Even if the other psychics slipped through his grasp, he wanted the destiny he came for.

## 12

Chance pulled his dusty truck into the driveway behind Turn of the Cards, and shut off the engine. The streets had been uncharacteristically deserted, and it made him anxious to get someplace safe for the moment. The back-of-the-house lights were still blazing, but the loading dock was sealed tight. Fortunately, he knew the code.

"Moira?" He carefully moved his shoulder where she'd fallen asleep. His beast had contentedly napped the whole way down to town, too, but was now alert. "We're here."

She sat up slowly and rubbed her face. "Ow." She touched her swollen nose and puffy eye with exploratory fingers. "Now I know what a mixed martial artist feels like after a fight. I don't even want to see a mirror right now."

"Let's get inside. I'll bring my first-aid kit." He pulled his backpack from behind the seat and looked around the backyard. He'd hoped to see Shepherd's reassuringly solid form, but it was awfully late.

"First, we call the sheriff, or whoever." She slid to the passenger side to grab her backpack from the floor.

A blur of movement and the scent of death were all the warning he had. He dove on top of Moira, shielding her from the shower of glass as three hundred pounds of frothing-at-the-mouth gray wolf slammed into the truck's driver-side window.

He felt a painful bite on his calf as the wolf tried to get in through the now-shattered window. The wolf lost its footing and slid back out. It jumped up on the truck's hood.

Chance needed to protect his mate, and knew he might lose her once she saw what he really was.

She was one step ahead of him. "Shift. Now." She started fumbling with the hem of his T-shirt.

"No need." He stilled her hand with his own. "But I'm big. Stay on the floor. Hide."

He opened his door as he reached for the shift and let the magic in his blood save his clothes. His human injuries melted away in the shift. It felt like it took forever, but he knew it was really under five seconds. The seat flattened alarmingly as his nearly eight hundred pounds of beast stressed its springs. He squeezed out of the open door and went on the hunt.

The wolf jumped off the truck and launched the psychic attack of a powerful alpha. *Submit!*

Chance's beast let the order flow past him as he stalked silently around the side of the truck. *Get bent, lapdog.*

The wolf growled his frustration and pressed the psychic attack harder, because some alphas were stubborn that way. The sound of paws on gravel said the wolf was positioning himself next to Moira's door.

Chance leapt up and over the truck to land in front of the big wolf. He struck with sharp claws, then followed up with a hard hit using his front paw, sending the wolf tumbling sideways, toward the loading dock.

*Stay down*, projected Chance, *or die like Richie did.*

*What the fuck are you?* Malevolent anger mixed with pissing fear in the wolf's scent. *I'll demand Shifter Tribunal judgment. You killed my pack!*

*Good luck with that.* Chance stalked closer, watching his prey. *Your twisted blood bond killed your pack. I just buried them.* Chance slowed and sniffed the rotting wolf. Without the stolen life essences, the alpha's body was falling apart by the minute. *You're next.*

*Not if you want your mate to live.* The thought was smug. He used an alpha half-shift to temporarily form guttural words. *"Now!"*

Chance heard the sound of a gun cocking and froze in mid step.

*You can kill me, or save your mate, but not both.*

Chance stayed still, scenting and listening, while watching the mangy gray wolf in front of him.

*See? This is why I tell wolves that true mates make them weak. And mating with a short-lived human, when we live for centuries? Stupid.* Pruhon rose and shook himself, dust and fur flying.

Familiar magic flared, but Pruhon didn't seem to notice.

*I'm leaving with my new recruits. You just stay here like a good...*

"Fuck!" The male voice came from somewhere high and to the right, beyond the fence into the next yard. "The truck disappeared."

Pruhon growled, then shouted. "Shoot where it was!"

Even as Chance leaped for Pruhon, a shot rang out and ricocheted off metal.

Chance got his massive jaws around the alpha's front shoulder and bit hard. The wolf yelped and tried to push away, but he was no match for Chance's teeth.

"Shoot!" Pruhon screamed, reinforcing it with an alpha command, and an undertone of panic.

Another shot rang out. Moira's magic flared again and stayed strong.

"Fuck! The light—I'm blind!" shouted the voice.

"Give me that, you idiot," said another voice. "Dad should have never given you that Ageless Assassin game."

"No! Get your own fucking gun." Sounds of a scuffle ensued.

Pruhon struggled to sink sharp canines into Chance's muzzle, so he bit down harder on Pruhon's shoulder, even though the putrid-tasting flesh threatened to gag him. The wolf's hind claws painfully raked Chance's belly, drawing blood.

Moira's voice rang out of nowhere. "Chance! He's got something small with stolen alpha power."

Chance forced the wolf to the ground with brute strength and put a serving-platter-sized paw on the wolf's ribs to hold him down. Chance blocked out all his beast's senses for a moment to locate the tiny magic pulse of power near the wolf's right hip.

Pruhon started twisting and squirming, and broadcast a desperate, vicious psychic blast that once might have felled a whole pack. *Die!*

Chance let the command roll on by and used his claws to flay open the wolf's flank. An impossibly clean pink gem gleamed where it sat embedded in the flesh. He dug it out with a claw and batted it away from the wolf's body.

The life essence that was Pruhon faded like the morning mist. His body began shriveling and aging at an incredible rate. The flesh caught in Chance's jaws sloughed away like a mouthful of decaying autumn leaves.

He backed away slowly, watching the body become a dry

husk that disintegrated and began drifting away in the cool mountain breeze.

"Huh."

He turned to see his mate and his truck materialize before him, like a special effect on TV. Moira watched the last of the late alpha's dust fly away, then turned to look at him. He stood stock still as she looked him over from head to tail. His nose worked to draw in the complex scent of his mate that held no hint of fear.

She frowned when her eyes lit on his stomach, where the wolf's claws had torn his skin loose. "Will shifting heal that?"

He hesitated, then nodded his big head once. So far, she hadn't reacted badly to him, but maybe she was just in shock. Even wolf, cougar, and grizzly shifters found him hard to be around.

She sighed and gave him a tired smile. "Then do it, you big looby, so you can kiss me and tell me everything's going to be all right." She pointed to the east with her thumb. "Besides, we have to call the sheriff and figure out how to get the Witzer wonder twins out of the neighbor's tree."

Outside of that one kiss and the too-short moment when he got to cherish her in his embrace, they were frustratingly never alone again.

Shepherd showed up just as Chance and Moira found a ladder. Moira's eyes grew round as she realized the eight-foot-tall hulk shaped like rocks on legs, with a grotesque face, was actually the helpful man from the garage.

"Sorry, I didn't mean to be rude." She shook her head. "I

wasn't seeing what was in front of me before. I'm going to have to figure out who everyone is again."

"That's okay. It's nice to be seen for what I am." He patted Chance on the shoulder. "I was worried about you. I'm glad you're okay."

Shepherd easily extricated Adam and Zed Witzer from the tall blue spruce, where they'd managed to get themselves hopelessly tangled in high-tech climber's rope. When questioned, they spilled everything. They'd agreed to help Pruhon capture and sell Moira if he agreed to change them into werewolves. As wolves, they'd be more powerful than their dad, and selling Moira would not only deprive him of something he wanted badly, it would make them rich. Their orders had been to shoot the truck's tires and engine, not Moira. After all, she was the merchandise.

Shepherd called the sheriff's office, and the dispatcher asked them to take their prisoners to the high school gym, where the occasional town hall meetings were held. Fortunately, Adam's errant shots had only gouged the body of Chance's truck, rather than hitting anything vital. Shepherd and Chance loaded the trussed-up twins into the back, and Chance and Moira drove them to the school. Chance had taken charge of the twins' rifle, which had dropped during their scuffle, and now had it safely secured in the pickup.

When they got there, a deputy sheriff named Shiloh handcuffed the Witzer boys and sent them off with a wolf-shifter officer to lock them in a patrol car. Chance and Moira followed Shiloh through the halls and gave him the Cliff Notes version of what had happened that night.

In the gym, nearly a hundred men and women sat on the wood floor, arms and legs secured with zip ties. Astonishingly, most wore silver jumpsuits, and some had metallic blue and green makeup on their faces. Except for the mix of irritated and glum expressions, and the number of pissed off fairies keeping watch, they could have been extras in a no-budget science-fiction movie.

"What the hell?" asked Moira, just beating Chance to the same question.

Shiloh laughed, displaying his permanently pointed coyote teeth. "I know, right? Some dimwitted outsider named Witzer thought he could get away with stealing psychics from Kotoyeesinay. He dressed his crew like alien invaders, so no one would believe the reports." He chuckled. "They even decorated some containment trucks to look like spaceships."

Moira shook her head in wonder. "How did you arrest so many people at once? If they're Witzer's goons, they all had tasers and guns."

"Oh, they did," agreed Shiloh, "and magic charms to make them seem like your best friend forever." His golden eyes gleamed with smartass humor. "They didn't believe in witches."

"I didn't, either, until last night... or was it this morning?" Moira blew out an exasperated breath. "I'm completely muddled. And are those floating creatures carrying scimitars?"

Chance put his arm around her and comforted his exhausted mate with a quick kiss. "The guards are djinn. They're part of the town's defenses. Witches can teleport."

Shiloh smiled. "The witches took the place of the real psychics and let themselves be put in the disguised trucks. When they got enough witches together, they teleported the mercenaries to the gym, and all the equipment to the town armory in Idyeria's demesne. She loves new toys."

"What did they do with the trucks?" asked Chance.

"Shepherd's salvage yard. He'll have them broken down in a couple of days, as if they never existed."

Moira frowned. "What about all these people?" She shoved her hands in the pockets of her hoodie. "They're mercenaries, but they have families. Lives."

Shiloh waved dismissively. "After we ask them a few questions, the elves will wipe their memories of ever having been here." He sighed theatrically. "I wanted to send them all to border-town drunk tanks, but the council said it would cause too much commotion."

"Are the elves going to make me forget, too?" Moira's forlorn tone made Chance's beast anxiously chuff inside him. Over his dead body.

Shiloh looked taken aback. "No, we'd never do that to people in need of sanctuary."

Moira was obviously floundering, and Chance knew it was his fault for letting her sleep on the way back down instead of telling her important things about the magic world. He tightened his arm around her and kissed the side of her head. "Let me take you home, and I'll explain everything."

"Not a good idea," said Shiloh. "We still haven't located Lawrence Witzer."

Moira's sudden tension made Chance's beast very unhappy.

Shiloh held up his hands. "Don't growl at the messenger. The oracles swear he hasn't left Kotoyeesinay, but no one has seen him. We think he's magically protected." He tilted his head toward the captives. "That's what we'll be asking them."

"He's never going to give up, is he?" Moira sighed. "I should leave. I've put everyone in danger. People could have been hurt."

Shiloh guffawed, startling a passing djinn into clinging to the ceiling. "You're kidding, right? We haven't had this much fun in years. We had to turn away volunteer 'psychics' for the invaders to capture."

"How did you find out about the invasion, anyway?" asked Chance. "That's what we were coming to warn you about."

"The council's oracles told us about the threat, but you know them, meaningful, but vague. It wasn't until we caught one of the video crews that we got the details."

It was Chance's turn to flounder. "Video?"

Shiloh pointed to a group of six people seated on the bleachers. "Witzer's sons found out about 'Operation Area 51' and hired the crews to get damning evidence on their father, not just for kidnapping the psychics, but for believing in them in the first place. They planned to use it to get their father declared incompetent and kicked off the board of his own company."

Moira heaved a sigh. "So if we can't go home, can I at least use a bathroom?" She looked at her filthy hands. "Train wrecks look better than I do at the moment."

Chance thought she looked more beautiful than the stars in the night sky, but he knew enough about women not to try convincing her. Instead, he pulled a travel pack of moist towelettes out of his vest pocket and gave it to her with a kiss.

She looked at the packet, then at him in disbelief. "You carry finger wipes?"

"Not usually." He shrugged. "They fell out of my tool bag. I forgot to put them back."

Shiloh asked one of the female reserve deputies, a young panther shifter from her scent, to show Moira the way there and back. Chance made himself stay put, but he couldn't help but follow her with his eyes until she was out of sight.

Shiloh gave Chance a sympathetic smile. "You got it bad, dude. Sometimes, I think mate biology is more of a hindrance than a help when it comes to shifters and love."

Chance shook his head. "I'm the only one of my kind, that I know of. I never thought it would happen to me."

Shiloh laughed. "None of us ever does, my friend. My husband is dozens of centuries old, and thought his mate was long dead, and I thought I was too broken from being a prisoner of war in Viet Nam. We danced around each other for a couple of years before admitting what our animals already knew."

"She's not a shifter. My pheromones are affecting her judgment."

Shiloh shook his head. "Don't let your fear mug your happiness in a dark alley."

His radio beeped, and he stepped away, leaving Chance alone with his thoughts.

## 13

One look in the mirror of the well-lit locker room told Moira she had unintentionally insulted train wrecks by comparing herself to them. Her right cheek was swollen, and her eye was turning a lovely shade of dark blue. Dried blood from her swollen, tender nose stained her chin and her T-shirt. Her stomach sported a fist-sized bruise from where Richie had slugged her. She stopped counting the various scratches, scrapes, and bruises. Her hair and clothes looked like she'd rolled down a mountain. Which, to be fair, she had, but that was beside the point.

She took off her hoodie, then made use of half of Chance's pack of towelettes, and asked her escort, a confident African American woman named Chantal, to help her brush the worst of the dirt off her back. Moira had a disconcerting moment when she looked at Chantal in the mirror and saw the unmistakable features of a black leopard. A quick glance at the real woman proved she hadn't shifted, so it was just Moira's magic, uncovering the hidden. She really needed to get a handle on that.

"You sure have that hot redhead shifter dancing a jig," commented Chantal. "If I were you, I'd reel him in fast."

Moira laughed to cover her embarrassment. "He's sinfully handsome, isn't he?" She carefully closed the pack of towelettes and slid it into the pocket of her hoodie. "Could I ask you a question? I'm new to all this, er, magical world stuff, and I'm still trying to understand everything."

Chantal shrugged. "Sure."

"Pruhon's wolves expected to get a lot of money by selling me at auction because I have magic and 'shifter-mate potential.' What is it? And is it only for wolves?"

"It's any shifter, usually. Some humans can successfully mate with a shifter, as in, make a soul connection and conceive cubs or pups or whatever. Good for avoiding inbreeding." She cocked her hip and rested her fist on it. "Some lazy-ass shifter outfits buy potentials like you and sex-mate them, rather than bother with all the courtship and consent stuff." She made a face. "Sex-mating is just what you think it is, except the mental bond never forms. My mama was sex-mated by a no-good leopard when she was a human and got accidentally pregnant. That didn't fit his plans, so he sold her to an auction, who sold her to a corrupt pride that planned to make her into a baby factory. Luckily, she escaped before he could force the shift change on her. Three months later, out I popped."

"Your mother sounds amazing. I've been running from a crazy man for three years. I can't imagine doing it pregnant. Or raising a child alone."

Chantal smiled. "My mom is alpha, through and through, but it would have sucked donkey balls if she hadn't met her true mate in an all-night truck stop. He may be a big grumpy bear, but he's the daddy of my heart."

Moira couldn't help but smile at Chantal's obvious affection. "How did the wolves know I have the potential?"

"Scent, usually. Did any of them lick your skin?" When Moira nodded, Chantal continued. "That's how. If I was attracted to women, your skin would taste sweet and spicy, make me want to eat you up."

Moira blushed when she remembered what she and Chance had done in the old bedroom at Turn of the Cards. Had that only been last night? She'd lost all track of time. Lack of sleep wasn't helping, either.

"So, this true mate thing. How does it work with shifters and humans?" She shrugged apologetically. "Don't answer if it's too personal."

Chantal chuckled. "This is a small town. Everybody's always up in everyone else's business. Those of us with enhanced senses know *exactly* who's been doing what with who." Chantal leaned against the counter. "My mama said it felt like sexual attraction at first, but it was deeper, like she wanted to hitch her wagon to his star and go wherever he did. She'd been so afraid, and he made her feel safe, even though they had both vengeful felines and coyotes hot on their tails. She'd been around plenty of shifters, and none of them ever made her hormones go off like the jackpot bells of a slot machine. They came here, the town granted sanctuary, and they got human-married a week later."

Chantal's radio beeped, startling them both. She tapped a button on the mic she wore on her uniform. "Chantal. What do you need?"

Moira heard tinny noise coming from Chantal's earpiece, but couldn't make it out.

"On my way."

Chantal stood up and smiled. "Come on, girlfriend. Your

redheaded shifter is making people nervous because he thinks you're hurt. Let's go show him you're finer than fine."

Moira's eyes found Chance the moment she entered the gym, right where he'd been. He was still the handsomest man she'd ever seen. And if she hadn't already fallen in love with him, his look of relief and slow smile as she crossed to him would have done the trick.

Chantal chuckled and leaned in confidentially. "If that man hasn't already chosen you as his mate, I'll go vegetarian for a week."

Moira's heart flushed with joy, but her brain knew they had some issues to deal with first. Starting with Lawrence Witzer. And her magic. And the fact that she was apparently a magnet to lazy-ass shifters who bought fertile females on shady Internet auction sites. Chantal peeled off to go handle an incident with some of the captives.

As soon as she got close enough, Moira took hold of Chance's outstretched hand. "We need to talk." She laughed when she realized they'd spoken simultaneously.

Chance snagged Shiloh as he walked by. "We need some privacy. Any place we can go?"

Shiloh smirked. "Should it have a sturdy horizontal surface?" He laughed at Chance's low growl. "The library has a room." He pointed to the gym's double doors. "Go right, past the intersection. First door to your left, then through the blue door marked 'Shhhh.'" He waggled his eyebrows. "You can play naughty librarian."

Chance growled again, but Moira just laughed. Shiloh was clearly incorrigible.

They found the room without trouble. It had six

separate study desks with laptop computers and headphones. Chance rolled out chairs for both of them, but sat close enough that their knees wove together.

She let herself marvel at his hazel-but-sometimes-amber eyes while she gathered her thoughts and her courage.

"I let Witzer ruin my life for three years because I thought my only talent was running. Then I broke down in Kotoyeesinay and met you, and you showed me my magic, and yours, and ours together, and now I don't want to run any more. I want to stand and fight. I want my life back because I have plans for it." She took his big, work-roughened hands in both of hers. "Plans that include you, if you'll have me. I love you, Chance McKennie."

He shook his head. "I need to tell you about shifters. Our pheromones are like an aphrodisiac to people with mate... some people." His thumb stroked hers. "I'm highly attracted to you, so my body might be putting your hormones in the driver's seat."

"Chantal told me about mates. I want you, sure, but that's only part of the package. You're smart, you're protective without being a jerk about it, and you could have any woman you want, and still you chose me." She smiled. "Besides, the big, blond, furry side of you is way beyond cool."

His head tilted quizzically. "You're not afraid of me."

"No." She studied his troubled face, trying to guess what he was thinking. "Should I be? I know we don't know each other very well yet, but you've shown me nothing but kindness and caring."

"My beast scares everyone. Even my parents. I had to leave to protect them, because her cougar pride and his wolf pack hated me." He said it like he was confessing to a dark, shameful secret. Her heart broke that people had hurt him so badly by rejecting the animal that shared his soul.

"Pffft," she said, waving dismissively. "That's because they've never seen a *Panthera leo atrox* in the flesh." She gave him a fierce smile. "Have you *seen* yourself? You're magnificent."

He blinked. "A what?"

"American lion. Ice-Age megafauna. Apex predator. Went extinct about eleven thousand years ago." She lifted one shoulder. "It took me a moment to recognize what you are. I helped excavate a skeleton in Florida for a guy looking to make a private sale. He got a graduate student to create an artist's interpretation of it, and the only thing she got wrong was your coloring and the thick muscles around your neck." Intuition, or maybe her magic, bubbled up. "I'll bet every mammal alive today has a genetic memory of being hunted by *P. atrox*. Ordinary shifters probably have a similar instinctive reaction to Ice Age shifters. You were all bigger and badder."

He pulled her out of her chair and into his lap, inhaling deeply as his arms encircled her. "I want to mate with you so bad I'm shaking." He kissed her with surprising tenderness. "But you have to understand, it's for life. We'll share a mental connection. I'll never cheat, because no other female will interest me." He brushed the bruised side of her face with his thumb. "You're human, so it's not the same. You can leave. You would, if you thought you were protecting me."

She bristled at the sadness in his tone, like he was giving up so she couldn't reject him like others had. "Two days ago, yeah, I would have left, because it's what worked before. Witzer is obsessed and ruthless, and I couldn't afford to make myself or anyone else vulnerable because I cared about them." She pulled back to make him look at her. "All it took was one kiss with you, and I knew I wouldn't leave, even if I should. I think that's why 'shifter-mate potential' is so valuable. Not just because I'm fertile with shifters, but because I can form the true-mate bond."

Even the thought of leaving his arms at that moment was enough to make tears threaten. "But I'll still be a magnet for the baby-factory auctions, and you'll outlive me by centuries, if what Pruhon said is true." She took a deep breath and let it out with a rush. "So here's the only solution I can come up with. Change me. Transform me into a bad-ass, Ice-Age shifter so I can mate with you for a very long life together, and kill anyone or anything that tries to get between me and my mate and our children. Cubs. Whatever." She swallowed, her mouth suddenly dry. "Your call."

It was hard not to fidget while she waited for his response. Despite her best intentions, insidious doubts began to creep in. Maybe she just *wanted* it to be the best thing for both of them, instead of *knowing* it to be true. Maybe he wasn't ready to change his independent lifestyle or share all of himself with someone else. Maybe he was as scared of her magic as she sometimes was. She couldn't do anything to stop the tear that fell.

His hold tightened on her. "Moira." He kissed her forehead and rocked her. "Claiming you will mingle our scents and take you off the baby-factory list. But you're right, I'll live longer than you if you stay human. I don't know what I did to deserve you, but I'm not giving you up."

She let herself be comforted in the soul-warming strength of the man who loved her, even if he hadn't said it. It had been a long damn night, and she hurt all over, except where he was holding her. She snorted with amusement through her tears. "Sorry about your shirt. Again."

"I told you, you can always cry with me." He stroked her hair. "You can be a bad-ass *Panthera leo atrox* shifter with everyone else."

Hope flooded through her and she pulled back to look at him, surprised to see his face was wet with tears, too. "You want this? You want me?"

He smiled and palmed her face. "How could I not?" He kissed her softly, but with the promise of so much more. "You're perfect."

Her hormones woke up in a flash, and she kissed him with passion, nibbling at his lips, loving the feel of his soft beard against her face.

He groaned and kissed her like he was starving. She loved how he teased her tongue with his, rather than trying to find out if she still had her tonsils. Her nipples hardened and competed with her core in demanding attention.

He tensed and pulled back. "Someone's coming."

She reluctantly slid off his lap and stood to face the door as it opened.

Shiloh grinned at them both. "We found Witzer."

Chance felt the tension in Moira as they stared through the one-way glass of the interrogation room in the sheriff's office. He slipped behind her and pulled her back to lean against him. She relaxed a little and voiced a small sigh.

The dripping wet, bedraggled man wearing a rubber-ducky inflatable life preserver around his waist didn't look like a monster. But neither had Pruhon. And Chance himself could be an eight-hundred-pound terror. No, a *Panthera leo atrox*. He liked having an identity.

Shiloh stepped up beside them wearing a shit-eating

grin, in sharp contrast to the patient neutrality he'd displayed for Witzer while in the small room.

"What did he tell you?" asked Moira warily.

"That he's suing us all, either before or after he sends the state police to arrest everyone in the town for theft, kidnapping, assault, and more theft. The theft really bothers him." Shiloh chuckled. "For all that he thinks he knows about the magical world, he doesn't believe half of what happened tonight."

Chance tightened his arms around his mate's waist. "Where did you find him?"

"In the outdoor dry sauna next door to Tinsel's. His plan was to break in, shoot Moira with a wolf tranquilizer, carry her to his limo, and head to the helicopter." Shiloh smirked. "His first mistake was hiding in Tinsel's sleigh when Shepherd came to the door."

"What does Tinsel's sleigh have..." Moira hesitated, then let her breath out. "Oh, her sleigh that actually *flies.*"

"Yup," agreed Shiloh. "It shot off into the night at eighty miles an hour and did about fifteen minutes of barrel rolls before dumping him into the swimming pool. Luckily for him, some kids were already in the pool, even though they weren't supposed to be, because he can't swim. Young Casey saved him by teleporting the life preserver on him and casting a spell so it lifted him six feet above the water. Casey couldn't figure out how to get him down, though, and the kids thought they'd get in trouble, so they hid him in the sauna, figuring the spell would eventually wear off."

Moira shook with laughter. "Then what?"

"Tinsel heard him shouting, and called us." Shiloh snorted. "He thinks the sleigh was picked up by a helicopter, and that he was held up by some sort of crane over the pool. He won't let us take the preserver off because it's evidence.

He doesn't trust, and I quote, 'the dumb-as-a-rock sheriff of a nothing-burger town' to handle it properly."

Chance shook his head. "So what are you going to do with him?"

Shiloh shrugged. "The usual, probably. Wipe his memory and send him on his way, along with his sons."

Moira pulled out of his arms to face Shiloh. "You can't do that."

Shiloh raised an eyebrow. "Why not?"

Moira waved toward the man sitting in the interrogation room grinding his teeth and drumming his fingers on the table. "He's a very rich, powerful man with dozens of public companies and even more shady deals with very dangerous people. If he's suddenly missing days from his memory, he'll hire people to track down what happened to him, and they'll find you." She started to shove her hands in her pockets, but grabbed Chance's hand instead. "All of you here are amazing, and powerful in your own right, but they'll keep coming because Witzer won't let it go. He's been obsessed with me for three years, chasing me for all over the continent for my magic. Think what he'd do to a whole town full of psychics, not to mention elves and shifters."

Shiloh's eyes narrowed in thought. "I wish the sheriff was here. I think I need to call the town council."

"I know you all don't know me from Eve, but I know how to derail him for good."

Chance felt the subtle flare of her magic, and he smiled. Her luck was about to tilt the universe in her favor, just like his own luck had brought them together. He squeezed her hand and smiled. She moved closer and leaned against his chest. "But first, could I go home with my mate-to-be and get cleaned up? I don't want to meet the council looking like a train wreck."

## 14

Chance was in heaven and hell. He and his mate were safe behind powerful wards, and comfortably cozy in Tinsel's castle's Lost Princess room, and she was in the shower. Through the steam, she smelled divine. His body thrummed with the need to join with Moira. But as much as he wanted to consummate their mating, they hadn't talked about having children, or at least so soon.

He'd insisted she use the bathroom first, then ran out to his truck get his own backpack with an extra set of clothes, and more importantly, condoms.

He was just putting his socks with his boots when she stepped out of the bathroom, gloriously and proudly naked, with a sultry gleam in her eye as she took in the fact that his jeans outlined his erection. His beast surged, and he panicked. He grabbed the towel from her hair and wrapped it around her and frantically thought human thoughts. The alarm code for Turn of the Cards. Stacking furniture in the extra bedroom. Breaking the bedpost when she'd given him the best oral sex he'd ever had. *Dammit.*

He scooped her into his arms and carried her to the wide canopy bed that looked like it had belonged in a fantasy dream sequence. He laid her out on the bed, then stepped back.

She rolled to her side and raised herself up on one elbow. "Chance, talk to me."

"I'm not in control right now. I don't want to hurt you. I have condoms." He rocked from one foot to the other, knowing he was sounding like a goofball again.

"I've seen your beautiful amber eyes before, and God, I hope I get to feel that tongue again. I have a birth control implant. The only way you'll hurt me is if you don't make love with me."

She pulled the towel off and cupped her breast with its stiffened nipple. Her words penetrated his desire-addled brain. Implant meant yes sex, no baby. He stripped, with no idea where his clothes went.

He crawled onto the bed and stalked his mate on hands and knees. She smiled and opened her legs in blatant invitation. "I've been dreaming of this." Her hands shaped the muscles of his arms and shoulders.

He swooped in for a kiss, remembering at the last second to avoid bumping her sore nose. He felt fleeting satisfaction of having killed the wolf that had done it, but rational thoughts dissolved when he tasted her. He kissed and licked his way to her beautiful breasts with their dark, tight nipples that delighted his tongue. Her moans of pleasure made his erection pulse in counter-rhythm. He continued his journey downward, noting each bruise he found and wishing he had magic to heal them with a kiss.

Her stomach was quivering by the time he got to the juncture of her splayed legs. He greedily licked the moisture he found there, then set about drawing more from her.

He borrowed a touch of his beast to lengthen and add texture to his tongue, then penetrated her core, enjoying the feel of her soft tissues clenching around him. He buried his nose in her pubic hair and filled his lungs with her scent. He was totally addicted to it. He was sure he'd need a fix at least once a day for the rest of his life.

He withdrew and entered her with his fingers, while his tongue found and caressed her swollen clit. Her inarticulate cries were almost continuous now as the tension in her clit increased. He scissored his fingers inside her, needing her to be ready, because his dick was so hard he could use it to pound nails.

"Make me come, Chance," she breathed. "Then make me yours."

He couldn't deny his mate.

Moira balanced on the edge of bliss, wanting both to savor the moment and succumb to the pleasure. But she needed him inside her, needed him to come inside her, needed to wrap her body and her magic around him.

He must have heard her plea, because his tongue unerringly found the perfect spot. He purred, and she was gone. Sharp pleasure made her whole body spasm, drawing noisy gasps from her throat. Another flick of his tongue sent a second wave crashing through her, arching her back in response.

He slid up her damp body, like he was marking himself with her sweat. She smiled at the intent look on his face and kissed him. "I love you." She reached between them and found his penis, moist at the tip and straining underneath. She raised her hips and guided him to her entrance.

His eyes turned fully amber as he sank slowly into her, their shared juices making the way slick and easy. His erection jerked in her, and her muscles clenched him in return.

"Give us what we both need, Chance. Make us one."

He growled and began thrusting, slowly and deliberately, kissing whatever his mouth could get to. She stroked his back and muscular butt with teasing fingertips, needing the weight of him on top of her and inside her to keep her from flying away.

His thrusts sped up, and she raised her legs to wrap around his. He began a sexy purr that sent a thrill through her. His lip curled away to reveal pointed teeth. She had a moment's trepidation about being bitten, but he shook his head rapidly, and the pointed teeth were gone.

The rubbing of his fiery red pubic hair against her clit was building another orgasm in her. She clutched his ass and urged him faster and deeper. His thrusts became erratic, and his purr turned into a growl. She slid her hand between them to feel the strength of him as he entered her, then moved to circle her clit with her fingertip. "Now, Chance."

He snarled as the first shock of bliss washed over her. His body stiffened. Powerful jerks of his penis inside her were followed by a warmth that began deep inside her and spread to her pelvis and up through her torso. Something in her reached for him and found two spirits, intertwined, opening to let her weave herself between them, becoming a solid single strand. The unearthly beauty of the shining cord that was their mate bond brought tears to her eyes.

*Now, we are one,* thought Chance. *You can't smell it yet, but my beast mingled our scents to make a new one that we share.*

*Good. I am yours and you are mine.*

She would have been content to drift there for hours, crooning to the big cat inside him and letting her magic dance over his human skin, as he wrapped her in the silk comforter and nuzzled her neck, purring. Unfortunately, the real world, in the form of both her and Chance's cellphones ringing out simultaneously, demanded attention.

She found hers first and answered, putting it on speaker.

*"Did I call at a good time?"* Shiloh asked, then laughed at Chance's growl. *"The council wants to hear Moira's plan for Witzer and company. They'll meet you for breakfast at the Blue Fairy in an hour."*

Chance frowned, and she felt his protectiveness surge.

"We'll be there," she said firmly, then ended the call. She palmed the scowling face of her true mate—she loved saying that—and brushed his cheek with her thumb. "If we don't deal with this now, we'll always be a target. Trust me, life on the run is the pits."

"I know. I got a sense of your plan from your mind, and it's clever." He kissed her palm. "Like you." He sighed. "I just don't like the risk to the woman I love."

She smiled and fought against tears. "I love you, too." Meeting the man of her dreams and mating with him had turned her into a watering pot. "Come share a quick shower with me so we can get dressed and face the world."

His eyes took on an amber glow. "I could lick you off afterward." It sent a zing to her core, and she knew he could feel it, too. She loved knowing how much he wanted her.

She stood and held out her hand to him. "Why don't we both do that for each other?"

## 15

Moira stood on the corner, waiting for her cue. She could feel Chance to her left, though he was concealed in the recessed doorway of Fantastic Faerie Frocks. She sent a pulse of love along their mate bond, which was apparently a palpable thing to every other shifter and magical creature they'd run across. She'd never been so congratulated in her life.

When the town council of Kotoyeesinay decided to do something, they went all in. Once again, they'd had to turn volunteers away for the little drama they were about to enact. Shiloh, in his native coyote form, but magically disguised to look like Pruhon's big gray wolf, would chase her down the street and catch her right in front of the sheriff's station, just as they were escorting Lawrence Witzer to his limousine. She'd pretend to stab Shiloh with her wicked-looking plastic knife, and he'd pretend to rip her throat out with his dying breath. Kotoyeesinay's elf elders would take care of the rest with magic.

Shiloh yipped once. Moira took off.

"Help! Help!" she shouted. She turned and looked over

her shoulder. Shiloh, with an overlay of huge, slavering wolf, was barreling toward her. So were nine other shifters of various species, each disguised to look like one of Pruhon's wolf pack.

A shifter wearing the Richie illusion brought back memories of his murderous rage, spurring her to run faster.

She pretended not to see the sheriff's station door opening and Witzer stepping out, with uniformed Chantal behind him.

Moira pretended to trip, then launched herself into the tumbling roll she'd learned from a bored stunt coordinator on the set of a movie she'd helped cater. The borrowed elbow pads, kneepads, and umpire's vest took the brunt of the impact, but it still stunned her for a moment.

*Stab me!* projected Shiloh, as he slowed and approached her with convincing menace.

"Pruhon, no!" shouted Witzer. "She's mine!"

Shiloh-as-Pruhon snarled defiantly at Witzer, giving Moira the perfect opportunity to stab at Shiloh's side several times with her plastic knife. Shiloh howled theatrically in terrible pain, then leapt on her and licked her neck wetly.

She screamed, then at the next lick, cut off her scream and stabbed one more time, then let her legs and arms go limp. She lolled her head to the side.

Shiloh's seventy pounds of furry weight dropped on her, nearly making her jackknife when his paw hit her bruised stomach and ribs. He sent her a wordless apology.

All around them, the rest of Pruhon's supposed pack began attacking each other and dying in spectacular and gruesome ways. Chantal jumped in, too, pretending to protect Witzer and be knocked down and savaged by her younger brother, an adolescent bear with a wolf overlay.

The real shifters were hamming it up, clearly having the time of their lives.

To Witzer, the street would look like a gory mess of blood, flesh, and dying wolves. He took the bait of seeing his limousine drive around the corner and made a dash for it, narrowly escaping the frenzied wolves that had gone insane at the death of their alpha. He waved his arms to get the driver to stop, then frantically launched himself into the passenger section. The limo tires screeched on the pavement as it peeled around a corner and made good its escape. Glade magic would help the limo find its way quickly out of town.

After several long moments, the street exploded with the laughter of eight naked men and women, including Shiloh. He fell off her and rolled into the side of an oversized jaguar that hadn't shifted. The jaguar licked Shiloh's face.

"Oh, goddess, did you see the look on his face?" wheezed Shiloh.

"No," said Moira as she sat up. "*Somebody* put his furry snout right on top of my head, and I couldn't move."

Chance and several others began distributing clothes to the naked shifters.

"It was just like you said," said Shiloh. "He thought he was the hero of the story, escaping with his life because destiny singled him out."

Chance helped her up and into his embrace with a lingering kiss.

"Come on, Matteo," Shiloh said to the big jaguar. "Shift naked and show everyone how smokin'-hot handsome my husband is. Make them all jealous."

Matteo turned out to be dark and suavely handsome, but Moira was much more interested in admiring her own mate. Too bad he wasn't naked, too. She kissed his chin. "Did the twins connect with their video crew?"

"Yes. We substituted the adjusted footage, gave them all memories to match about spending all night filming Witzer and editing the video, and sent them and their van toward Cheyenne, where there's a TV station with a satellite uplink."

"Good," said Moira. "Witzer will be ruined, one way or the other. His sons will probably destroy the empire inside a year."

A pair of older, plump women came out of the sheriff's station. "Did we do good?" asked one. Their masking magic faded to reveal two pointy-eared, green-skinned dryads who wore leaves and flowers for clothing.

Chantal crossed to them. "Perfect, Adjaini. Thanks to Witzer 'accidentally' overhearing you as 'Jane,' he thinks all the psychics in Kotoyeesinay are scam artists with a bunch of stage tricks to fool the gullible."

"It's like I said when I first got here," said Moira with a laugh. "Best tourist gimmick ever."

Chance slipped his hand into hers. "Iolo Maxen's back in town and wants to see us."

Her eyes widened with dismay. "Oh no, did we leave a mess at the store?"

He smiled. "No, everything's fine. He says he brought you something from Laramie."

She raised an eyebrow. "Better not be another kitten. One Pandora is quite enough."

Mr. Maxen let them in through the front door, then locked it behind them. His real visage was an ethereally handsome elf, an iron-and-silver-colored version of the blond elves from the movies, and the differently handsome golden elves of the town council. She could see how his illusion charm had made his features plainer and skin tone look human. The Edwardian-style jacket was totally him.

The mirrors winked at her as they threaded their way through the aisles toward the back, and she smiled. She loved the feel of the magical objects, and the net of power woven into the building itself. Chance smiled at her when she slowed to caress one of the little mirrors.

Mr. Maxen paused at the wide, doorway to the workshop. "Will you be comfortable, Ms. Graham?"

She smiled widely. "I'm seeing everything, sir, including the magic built into the hieroglyphics on the door. Feels like security."

Since mating with Chance, she'd gained a measure of his super-sensitivity to the various flavors of magic. He'd said his own free magic felt more accessible, too.

The corners of his mouth lifted. "Very good, Ms. Graham."

He led them to the back entrance, and pointed to a small box on the cart. "This is atonement for my bad behavior during the first two days of our acquaintance."

"Your... I don't follow." She sent a puzzled glance to Chance, but he shrugged.

Mr. Maxen clasped his hands together in front of him. "I experimented with your magic without your consent. At first, I didn't believe you didn't know about it, that you were hiding it on purpose for some nefarious purpose. Imposters have asked for sanctuary before. Once I realized you truly had no idea what you had or how powerful it is, I tested your scope and strengths. It was... unkind." He looked abashed. "Mr. McKennie told me at lunch that my little experiments made you think you were dying of a brain tumor."

She waved off his apology. "The flickering was driving me batty, I'll admit, but it started almost the moment my car died in front of the diner." She glanced at her redheaded mate. "Actually, from the moment I was lucky enough to meet Chance." She smiled at him as she slipped her hand into his, then turned back to Mr. Maxen. "He calls it my 'just-in-time' magic."

"A fair assessment, but we'll get to that in a minute. I should have guessed your first visit to the workroom would be unpleasant, but I hadn't understood the nature of your dual talents."

She snorted. "I'm glad one of us understands it. Why did you experiment on me in the first place?"

Mr. Maxen gazed at his feet. "I am a scholar of magic and a tinkerer, Ms. Graham. You presented a unique opportunity to test my theory that disbelief can suppress or obfuscate inherent magic, but that magic always finds a way to work."

Moira was intrigued, in spite of having been a test subject. "How do you separate coincidence from magic?"

"Usually, intention and repeatability," said Mr. Maxen. "You have knowing magic, the ability to see the hidden truths, and hide them as well. But the fundamental power of your stronger magic, like Mr. McKennie's, is influence. Colloquially, luck." He raised an eyebrow. "Individually, you are each an influencer of unlikely occurrences. Together— congratulations on your mating, by the way—you are a nexus for significant change. Confluence magic is rare and can be very powerful."

"Huh." She didn't know what to make of that. "So, that's, er, good?"

Chance rumbled a little as he pulled her closer to him and sent a pulse of reassurance along their mate bond.

Mr. Maxen shrugged one shoulder. "Change begets both winners and losers." He picked up the box and held it. "One more question. What do you know of your biological parents?"

"Nothing of my dad, except his name, and he was Canadian. You'd think a name like 'Zephyr Atsingani' would be an easy find on search engines, but knowing my mother, he was probably a child of a sixties commune and thinks technology is evil. My only legacy from him is dual citizenship in Canada. My mom was Cherry Graham. She died of a heroin overdose when I was twelve." Actually, her mother had checked out of life a lot sooner than that. Moira had learned to cook, clean, and get herself to school by the time she was nine.

Chance stirred. "You told me you used your mother's last name at the Ren fair. You must have kept using it, once you realized Witzer was after you."

She nodded. "It was the only way I could think of to keep my foster parents out of the whole mess. They're good people, and loved me, even when I was a sullen Goth girl with serious trust issues. Bad foster-care stories make the headlines, but there are a lot of success stories like mine." She shook her head. "But I have to admit, they're very practical, down-to-earth people, and never knew what to make of me." She sent a thread of magic to flash a beam of light from a nearby mirror. "Now I know why."

Chance squeezed her hand. "Show off." She grinned.

Mr. Maxen handed her the box. "This is your paternal heritage."

She opened the box's hinged lid to reveal an antique, leather-bound book tied with a blue ribbon, an old tintype photograph, and underneath, a round, silver-framed mirror. The silver was black with tarnish, but the mirror was clear, though wavy, as if the glass was handmade. The old, white-haired man in the photograph had a thick, white mustache and wore a puffy-sleeved shirt and an ethnic vest covered with mirror embroidery.

"Your paternal grandfather," said Mr. Maxen. "He was a noted sorcerer in his day. He'd be called Romani now, though they were known as Atsinganoi back when I was in the emperor's court. Traveling fortune tellers and wizards. The mirror and the journal were his."

"How did you find this?" She caressed the corner of the book with her thumb. "How did you even know where to look?"

"I'm over two thousand years old. I knew your great-great-great grandfather. His gift with mirrors was very like yours. He was a master of hiding the seen and uncovering the hidden, and of knowing the truth. He fell in love with a banshee, as I recall, because the curse couldn't hide her beauty from him." Mr. Maxen smiled sardonically. "He was also an inveterate gossip who had to make hasty exits more than once because he shared his juicy tidbits with the wrong person."

"And the rest?" she asked, tilting her head toward the box.

"I called a few old acquaintances and cashed in a favor. We serious collectors of *objets magiques* all know each other. These were what I could find quickly. There may be more."

She touched the mirror because it called to her, which reminded her of the little mirror she'd broken but had saved her anyway. She handed the precious box to Chance, then pulled out the brass frame from her back pocket. She unwrapped its bandanna covering and held it out to Mr. Maxen. It looked sad with only one corner of mirror left.

"I found this in your backyard, and it broke when Richie jumped me. How much do I owe you for it?" She hoped it wasn't too high, or she'd be paying it off forever.

He picked it up and examined it with his fingers and eyes. "Nothing. It's not mine."

"It's magic, though, isn't it?" She frowned. "Can it be fixed? Maybe I can find the owner."

Mr. Maxen shook his head. "The only magic I sense in it is yours. Otherwise, it's just an old shaving mirror that yellowed with time."

Chance put a hand on her shoulder. "Just-in-time magic, remember? You needed it to get out of the cave, and your magic found a way. The wolves even let you keep it because it looked like a broken tourist trinket."

"Huh," she said, for lack of anything more cogent. She needed time for thinking.

Chance turned to Mr. Maxen. "Did you find the charm I told you about?"

Once again, she was lost.

"Yes, right where you said it would be," Mr. Maxen replied. "Nasty piece of work, that. I've locked it in the shielded vault for now. Stolen alpha power is extremely valuable on the black market."

"You're talking about the small thingie that was in Pruhon's ass?" At Mr. Maxen's nod, she continued. "It was weird, sensing its presence and having the knowledge sort of pop into my head. I didn't even know what alpha power was until I felt it. And when Pruhon was fighting Chance, I got the impression that the witch who made it did it out of revenge, but I don't know for what. It felt really ancient. Centuries, maybe." Realizing what she'd said to a two-thousand-year-old elf, she hastily added, "Not ancient. Mature. Seasoned. Experienced."

"Ancient will do, Ms. Graham. It is, after all, the truth as far as humans understand it." He crossed his arms. "Do you have any questions?"

"So many, I can't think of any of them," she said ruefully. "Except one. What's a 'demesne'? An estate or something? That's where Shiloh said the djinn guards came from, and where the town armory is."

"They are lands in a different plane. Fairies create them." He tilted his head thoughtfully. "Think of them as cul-de-sacs of other dimensions that are glued to this one by gateways. The glade is full of them." He waved a circling finger. "My workroom is a modified version of a tiny demesne, so the accumulation of magic from these objects doesn't tempt anyone."

"Glade?" She shook her head. She had so much to learn, and maybe unlearn, too.

Mr. Maxen smiled. "Sort of like the wards on this building, but on a much larger scale. Elves can pool their magic to create a perimeter. They tie themselves to the land, and the land to them. They draw strength from the land and living things, and protect them in return. This glade was created in the early 1800s by a company of like-minded elves and their paramours, who were fleeing their own disapproving clans, and a cabal of English alchemists who wanted their magic. They first offered sanctuary to fairies and other magic users in need who could also help defend the glade. Now, we're a beacon of hope in this part of the world. Kotoyeesinay is one of the more diverse sanctuaries on the continent, probably because the New World attracted the adventurous."

"Like you?" asked Chance. She could tell he was guessing, but it felt right.

"Perhaps." Mr. Maxen raised one shoulder slightly. "Many of us here are unique, and don't fit in elsewhere."

"What did the Native Americans think of all this?" Moira asked. "This valley seems like prime summer camping ground to me."

He laced his fingers together. "The town founders came to an understanding with both the Arapaho and the Ute." He frowned. "To our shame, we did not do well by our accommodating friends. We thought it enough to warn them not to trust the government's negotiators, and did not stop the Army from forcibly herding our proud allies into the Utah territory, like they were wild horses to be broken and penned." He sighed. "That's why we made the valley into a reservation land trust and built the casino. Its profits fund tribal scholarships. It's our atonement."

"I respect that." She appreciated people who admitted a mistake and tried to make up for it.

Mr. Maxen gave her a considering look. "Will you stay in Kotoyeesinay, do you think?"

She looked to Chance, then back to Mr. Maxen. "We'll have to get back to you on that, but I'll be here on time tomorrow, if you still need my help in the shop." She pointed to the ceiling. "And we'll finish your guest quarters."

His mouth twitched with a smile. "Very good, Ms. Graham."

# EPILOGUE

Chance lay naked on the bed, staring up at the stars painted on the canopy above him and Moira, sated and relaxed. The August weather had been unreasonably hot that week, and the high, dry winds required constant vigilance for wildfires. Kotoyeesinay's glade magic couldn't protect the whole mountain range, so physical methods were needed, including superior shifter senses and strength.

Tinsel's magical frosty air conditioning offered welcome comfort, especially after the pleasurable exertion of making love. His poor mate needed the cool air just as badly— female *Panthera leo atroxes* were designed for the Ice Age, too.

He'd been terrified he'd screw up her change, and made Shiloh and his husband, who turned out to be a jaguar demigod from South America, stay on call until he was sure she'd made the transition and would thrive. Her beast was the noblest creature he'd ever seen, and she took to four-footed movements with amazing speed and grace.

"Alaska." He heard the yawn in her word.

He shook his head. "Too political. Wolves and bears are constantly fighting over dwindling resources, they victimize the caribou shifter clans, and they all think they're too good for the native humans. And if the oil rigs come back, it'll stink on ice."

She snorted. "You're a punny man." She intertwined her fingers with his. "Where do you want to go?"

"Michigan Upper Peninsula. Introduce me to your foster parents, so they see I'm not a monster and quit worrying so much."

"It was just the one email. I think they were afraid I'd joined a cult or something. I couldn't very well tell them we're staying in Kotoyeesinay because the elves granted me sanctuary so I can learn magic, and get better at turning into a prehistoric beast who could catch and eat a moose for breakfast." She sighed. "How long has it been since you've seen your parents?"

"Fifteen years. I miss them, but in shifter years, that's like last week. I doubt anything has changed in the cold war between the cougars and the wolves, and *two* Pantheras in their midst would be like throwing a lighted match on gasoline."

She was quiet for a long while.

"Maybe," she said thoughtfully, "we should quit trying to fly against the wind, and just go where our luck blows us, as long as it's someplace north. I don't think I could stand anywhere warmer, now that I can get furry. Iolo's remodeling is done, and Tinsel is losing money for this room because she won't let us pay her." She rolled onto her side and rested her head on his shoulder. "If we come back by winter, maybe we could find our own place, farther away from the other shifters, so we don't make them so nervous. Maybe even build a house, if we trade our finding magic for someone's conjuring magic." She chuckled. "With what Iolo overpaid us, we could build a mansion. He really has no sense of money."

It was his turn to be quiet. "I'd like that. I've been traveling so long that I never even imagined owning a house and land."

"Me, either. I used to think I was born without the nesting gene that most women seem to have." She kissed his chest. "Turns out, I just needed to find the right someone to nest with." She put her hand on his chest. "But I still want to go north. We could just drive there and see what there is to see."

"You're okay with that? I thought women liked itineraries and stuff."

"I'm part Romani. Apparently traveling is in my blood, if my grandfather's journal is anything to go by. The open road called to him."

He pulled her closer. "I love you." He sent the depth of emotion behind his words over their mating bond. He didn't say it often enough.

"You don't have to say it, love." She draped her leg over his and patted her hand over his heart. "I feel it."

Chance stretched out his new, stronger magic to turn off the bedside lamp, leaving them bathed in moonlight from the skylight. He was learning his magic just as Moira was learning hers. He took a long moment to savor the luck that had brought him his destiny. His Moira.

The painted canopy of stars reminded him of his childhood home, where the nearest city lights were hundreds of miles away. "How about the Northwest Territories in Canada?" Big, and far enough away from the Yukon to keep his parents safe. Arctic air, trees, mountains, good hunting. He'd enjoy introducing his mate to the simple animal joys of chasing snowshoe rabbits and hunting by moonlight.

A subtle wave of confluence magic washed over him.

"Fort LeBlanc," she said sleepily.

"What?" He turned to look at her, but her eyes were closed.

"We have to help the dire wolves."

Thank you for reading *Shift of Destiny*, the second story in the Ice Age Shifters series. If you liked it, please post a quick review, so other readers can enjoy it, too.

There are more stories in the Ice Age Shifters series. Sign up for my newsletter at http://bit.ly/CVN-news so you won't miss finding out about new books.

Thanks to my brave and honest beta readers and typo hunters, my professional editor Shelley Holloway, my talented cover designer Amanda Kelsey, and my equally talented sketch artist Sam Salas.

The Ice Age Shifters series:

- *Shifter Mate Magic (Book 1)*
- *Shift of Destiny (Book 2)*
- *Heart of a Dire Wolf (Book 3)*
- *Dire Wolf Wanted (Book 4)*

# FREE EXCERPT FROM HEART OF A DIRE WOLF (ICE AGE SHIFTERS BOOK 3)

LOCATION UNKNOWN ~ AUTUMN ~ PRESENT DAY

Skyla Chekal wrinkled her nose when she got a whiff of herself as she rolled over on the thin pad to face the cell bars. Despite the forceful ventilation system, despite periodic hose-downs, and despite the heavy-duty suppression spells and magical dampeners, prison stank.

She was definitely adding to the stench. The shapeless gray sweatpants and loose T-shirt issued to her clung to her in uncomfortable places. She desperately needed a thirty-minute hot shower to wash off the pervasive odors of fear, rage, despair, and confinement stress. She was lucky. Unlike most shifters, she could tolerate small, enclosed spaces for long periods. She'd have never completed her doctorate without being able to practically live in classrooms and libraries, some a lot smaller than her thirteen-by-nineteen-foot holding cell.

Every high-pitched whine of a miserable fairy or keening shifter increasingly grated on her nerves. The magical sound dampeners had obviously been designed and cast by wizards with normal human hearing. It apparently hadn't occurred to them that shifters and other magical creatures had a wider range.

None of the unwilling guests she'd talked to in the underground complex had any idea where in the world they all were, and she'd lost track of time. She didn't know if it had been four weeks or five since she and her older sister Rayne had been ambushed in a Los Angeles alley.

It had been only chance that she and Rayne were together at all. Rayne's job as an investigator took her away from her Los Angeles apartment more often than not, and Skyla lived in Santa Barbara while she finished her doctorate. She'd driven to L.A. for a dinner with Rayne to celebrate the submittal of her dissertation just that morning.

Getting her doctorate was the first big milestone on her plan for a teaching career mixed with research. If she lived through this, she hoped the university would grant her an extension for missing her dissertation defense appointment. Not every student could say they'd been kidnapped to be sold into magical slavery.

She'd only glimpsed Rayne a few times since awakening in the sterile exam room and being shoved in a cell, and she worried about how her active, outdoorsy, do-it-now sister was handling being caged. Their jailers did everything possible to keep their magical prisoners off balance and under control, including shuffling cell assignments, and unpredictable schedules for feeding time and lights out. The trips to the auction block, where shifters were poked, prodded, bullied, and sometimes bloodied by prospective buyers, seemed equally random.

In the semi-darkness, Skyla inched herself as close as she dared to the dangerous bars. Their magical punch could knock her out for hours, but she'd discovered that very power created a neutral zone for some of the suppression spells. Knowledge had power of its own. The more she knew about the magical protections, the mix of human and non-human guards who had defensive spells and weapons galore, and what kinds of shifters were in the holding cells, the better chance she had to reunite with her sister and escape. Skyla wasn't fearless or a natural leader like Rayne, so even if she could figure out how to escape her cell, she couldn't leave without her sister.

And, if the moon goddess cared anything for the lives of individual shifters, Skyla also wasn't leaving without her mate.

At least, she thought that singular, toe-curling, breathtaking scent had to be that of her mate. It was just like her mated friends described—the most attention-getting, enticing scent in the world, that made her want to roll in it, until it saturated every cell in her body. That made her want to jump his bones before even finding out his name. That made her ready to embrace whatever species he was.

Because, of course, the *best possible* time to run across one's true mate was as a prisoner, under constant threat of death or worse, and looking—and smelling—like something a buzzard stole from a lizard.

She'd moved her sleeping pad close to the deadly bars just to catch occasional whiffs of that scent. She was pretty sure her mate was male, because while she liked women, she'd never desired sex with them. She wished she knew what he looked like, or at least knew his name, but she'd take what she could get. She was fortunate; some shifters went centuries, or even a lifetime, without ever finding a mate. Her well-hidden inner beast stopped its near-constant howling whenever she smelled his scent, and she even managed a few hours of sleep when the overhead lights were out.

From the far back corner of her cell, she heard the low-pitched growl of her latest roommate. The guards who'd shoved her into the new cell warned her that, despite his pronounced palsy, he was feral—human-shaped but with the mind of his beast—and dangerous.

She had the impression he'd been captive for a long time. Apparently, no one had wanted to buy a shifter who couldn't talk, shook like he was having a seizure, and couldn't be forced to shift into his animal shape. Bad dreams visited Lerro often, and the guards kept him drugged to the eyeballs and magically compelled just to get him to and from the auction block without a knock-down, drag-out fight.

To honor Lerro's bravery and stubborn defiance, she'd been sharing what little magic she could spare to help his own shifter strength counteract the drugs and fight off the compulsion spells. She sent him a thread now, too low-level to trip the multiple magical alarms, but enough to help him relax into dreamlessness. She wished Rayne was there to help. She'd know what to do.

Skyla stayed still for as long as she could bear it, using her magical senses to investigate the set of spells that controlled the cell doors. She'd never met another shifter with as much free magic as she had, and she hid it well, so the slave traders' intake staff hadn't noticed her talent. She'd worked out the rest of the spells in place in the prison area and knew how to unravel them quickly, but the door spells were cleverly linked to the central monitoring room and the identity charms and weapons the staff carried. She needed one of each to be sure she could break them all, and sadly, the guards weren't cooperating by carelessly leaving them behind for her to study.

She finally sat up, frustrated from wanting to be enveloped by the man who owned that scent, and her human form aching from the cold that radiated from the concrete floor. She considered shifting, but as stressed as she was, she couldn't be sure her illusion would hold for any length of time. Her true beast could tolerate being far colder. Since being captured, she'd only shifted once using her illusion, and briefly, to avoid a cattle prod. The auctioneers thought they were selling a shy, skittish South American maned wolf.

She and Rayne had improved the illusion spell over the years, to where it was almost built into the marrow of their bones, but it hadn't been designed to be undetectable to prying wizards. Remedying that was high on her project list, right after breaking out with her mate and her sister and getting as far away as possible. Visualizing her goals helped keep paralyzing fear and spiraling worry at bay.

The harsh overhead lights hummed and blinked on. She stood and stretched, then crossed to the small plastic sink and cold metal toilet. She used the toilet, then drank from the sink and rinsed off her face. She finger-combed her filthy hair, which felt like a bird's nest.

It hadn't taken her long to figure out the auctioneers weren't selling shifters for their beauty; they sold them for their inherent strength. Humans with shifter-mate potential got showers, soap, and new clothes to make them attractive to shifter groups who were too incompetent or corrupt to find mates on their own. Shifters, if they were unbearably stinky, got sprayed down with industrial hoses. She knew that better than most. Before she'd been separated from her sister, she'd tweaked their illusion spells to make them both smell subtly of decay and rot. She'd been hosed down eight times since her arrival, after would-be buyers complained.

So far, she and Rayne had managed to keep their secrets, but every new day increased the likelihood that some asshole wizard would take a closer look.

She rolled up her thin sleeping pad and stowed it on the narrow ledge at the back of the cell, per the rules. She approached her roommate and extended her toe cautiously to nudge his outstretched foot. "Lerro."

He gave a half-snort and turned his head. A shudder racked his torso.

She nudged harder. "Rise and shine."

Lerro sat up in a blur of motion, snarling through unnaturally elongated teeth and striking out with fists and feet. Expecting it, Skyla jumped out of the way. She hadn't been fast enough the first time. Her jaw had hurt for hours.

He'd growled and glared at her every day since, but she refused to treat him like an animal. "You just aren't a morning person, are you?" She pointed toward the cell door. "Unless you want to miss feeding time at the zoo, get up." The guards only offered meals to awake, human-shaped, compliant prisoners.

Lerro hissed at her, but the effect was ruined when he yawned. He clumsily rolled up his pad and put it on the ledge.

She watched as he stumbled toward the sink. He seemed to be moving better than he had been before lights-out, after another failed trip to the auction block. She belatedly wondered if she was doing him any favors by helping him with her magic. If he seemed more alert and less damaged, someone might take a chance and buy him.

She turned away to give him the illusion of privacy, even though shifter senses left little to the imagination. Every shifter was always aware of the private business and intimacies of others, whether they wanted to be or not.

A phantom magical sensation alerted her to the proximity of her sister. Relief flooded her, because it had been much fainter for the last week, like when Rayne had been in Kenya last year. When they'd been young and untamed, their parents had traded with a golden elf in Wyoming for a magical locator link between all four of them. Her mother was dead, and their father had vanished off the face of the Earth two years ago, but the link still worked between her and Rayne.

When she heard the chains of the shackles, she moved close to the bars. The shadow spells that blocked prisoners from seeing into the nearby cells didn't block their view of the wide corridor.

Shock froze her at her first glimpse of Rayne, who was surrounded by four guards and trailed by a fifth. Her sister looked like a feral version of herself, with unkempt frizzy hair, a bloody nose, and torn sweats with visible bloody whip welts underneath. Nothing sane remained in her half-shifted, solid brown eyes.

Skyla whimpered. "Rayne..." Only the painful warning tingle stopped her from reaching through the bars.

A husky guard accidentally stepped on the trailing chain of Rayne's ankle shackles, causing her to stumble.

A dark-skinned, black-haired guard thumped her hard on the hip with a metal nightstick. "Bad dawg!"

In a flash, Rayne crouched and grabbed the nightstick with both hands, then used it to ram the guard's belly. He folded and collapsed, but two other guards attacked in practiced unison, each going for Rayne's knees with their batons. Rayne dodged by jumping, as if the heavy shackles weighed nothing.

The trailing guard, a sadistic creature with tusks, horns, and an armored hide, hurled a sparkling magical fireball into Rayne's back. Magical shockwaves sparked against the cell bars up and down the corridor. Rayne grunted and fell to her knees. She bared her elongated teeth and growled a bone-chilling threat. Shifters up and down the cell block howled.

Skyla clenched her fists. "Rayne, stay down!" She couldn't use magic to help, or she'd set off the alarms.

Rayne sprang to her feet and grabbed the heads of the two human guards, then rammed them together and slammed them to the floor.

Caged shifters cheered when Rayne bent a metal nightstick and used it to hook the arm of the hated, thick-hided guard. The fireball the guard had been about to cast skittered across her own armored skin like lightning, leaving a chaotic pattern of scorch marks on her arm and chest. The guard roared louder than a freight train. More guards appeared to wade into the fray.

In the end, it took eight fully-armed guards to subdue one maddened shifter who had finally lost herself to mindless instinct.

Skyla dropped to her knees in helpless horror as the guards continued to savagely beat her sister into a barely recognizable mass of blood spray and broken bones. The final blow was a fireball that left a blackened scorch mark on Rayne's stomach as her T-shirt burned away.

The tiny magical connection between Skyla and her sister faded to nothing.

A guard bent to check the carotid pulse, then shook his head.

The blood-spattered, armor-hided guard held out her hand with another sparking fireball in her palm, glaring triumphantly at each of the cells. "Who elssse wantssss to die?"

From deep within the heart of Skyla's beast arose an implacable rage, drawing her to her feet. She shuffled slowly backward to the far back wall of the cell. Taking two centering breaths, she focused all her attention on the bars as she gathered her carefully hoarded magic. Once she blasted through the bars, she would show the guards what she really was...

The next thing she knew, Lerro tackled her to the floor. With his full weight on top of her, he hissed softly in her ear. "Do not die."

She snarled at him. "Let me go!" She borrowed her beast's strength to buck him off so she could twist away.

He tackled her again and put his mouth next to her ear. "No one to live for?" His body shuddered, but he held on. "No friends?" His words were more breath than sound. "No mate?"

A powerful scent memory flashed through her, piercing the blind, black anger of her berserk beast. If she succeeded in killing the armor-hided creature, the guards would kill her as a warning to the others. Then she'd never even find out if her mate felt the call, or if he liked snow, or tasted as divine as he smelled. Her sister had died before ever finding her true mate. How could Skyla throw away her own chance?

Lerro must have felt her relax, because he rolled off her and crawled away. He fell onto his side, trembling and panting.

Rage and loss threatened to drown her, so she turned her focus to Lerro. She wasn't all that surprised to learn he could talk. She very badly wanted to pepper him with a million questions, but that would expose one of his secrets.

A loud clatter from the corridor had her climbing to her feet. Everyone in the shifter holding cells knew that sound. "Oh look, the maids are here."

Within minutes, a pair of guards dragged a four-inch hose in front of their cell. "Hug the walls. Now!"

She and Lerro flattened themselves against opposite walls. The guards opened the valve to unleash a forceful spray of soapy water onto the cell's floor. Her bare feet ached from the cold. Lerro caught her eye, a newly intelligent gleam in his. He looked to the guards, then back to her again. A shudder racked him, and his eyes rolled back in his head.

Skyla looked at the burly human guards. As usual, it took two of them to hold the hose steady so it didn't buck like a bronco. As usual, the water had a bit of magic mixed in with the soap and smelled of chemicals and metal. What was she supposed to be looking at?

She was about to risk a questioning glance at Lerro when it hit her. She'd seen it a dozen times and never thought about it. The magic of the bars should have repelled the water but didn't.

She opened her magical senses wide and sent low-level probes to test the bars and the water, to see how they worked together. Unlike most of the lazy, brute-force spells she'd encountered in the underground prison, the interconnected security spells for the cell bars and doors were subtle and elegant. She sure as hell didn't want to meet the dangerous and gifted wizard who'd created them.

She made herself look away, as if uninterested. Lerro was very much more than he seemed. She owed him twice, once for showing her the water magic, and once for preventing her from committing suicide.

Skyla wasn't the right person to plan a great escape, but

with Rayne gone, she'd have to do. She still planned to avenge Rayne's death and do as much damage to the prison as possible, but she'd do it on her terms, and help as many people as she could in the process. Only together did they have a chance at freedom...

Continue the adventure in Heart of a Dire Wolf